"Gonzagini"

by
Donald H. Jans

FADE IN:

SUPER: MALTA AIRPORT 1987

INT. AIRPORT - MALTA - MORNING

A tanned HAND places a SILVER TOSHIBA BOOM BOX on a black
rickety conveyor belt. The yellow florescent tag on the
boombox reads: AIR MALTA: SEATTLE VIA LONDON. 80's NEW WAVE
MUSIC seems to blare from the turned off boom box.

INT. BOCCA LUPO RESTAURANT - FLORENCE,ITALY - EVENING - 1987

SUPER: FLORENCE, ITALY

Ninety college students, the GONZAGINIS, dressed to the nines
in overly colorful 80's wear, revel in their boisterous
farewell dinner at the posh street-level restaurant.

The same NEW WAVE MUSIC forces HENRY (20) a strapping blond,
to yell to his best friend TOM (20) a surfer dude, and Tom's
curly haired, tough-as-nails girlfriend, KATE (20), while
they hold their tequila shots.

A banner above reads: FAREWELL GONZAGINIS

                    TOM
          Salute ai Gonzaginis.

Henry and Tom slam their tequila shots and shudder. Kate
tosses hers over her shoulder and winks at Henry.

                    HENRY
          Man, I'm gonna miss you guys.

Just then, STEPHANIE(20), a fresh-faced effervescent redhead,
plants a wet kiss on Henry. He welcomes her.

                    STEPHANIE
          You're going to see them in three months.

Stephanie waves her hand in front of her mouth to fan the
alcohol from Henry's kiss.

                    HENRY
          I know, but it's not going to be the
          same.

NELLA(20) a large boned, overly made-up brunette in expensive
clothes, goes in for her own hug.

                    NELLA
          I'm gonna miss you too, even though
          you're an asshole.

Nella hugs Henry. Stephanie beams at them like a proud mother.

On a makeshift stage behind them, BRUNO(40) a handsome priest dressed in street clothes and Birkenstocks pats a laughing girl on the back holding a certificate. As she leaves the stage, Bruno slyly checks out her butt.

                    BRUNO
               (Italian accent)
          And for the "Ugly American Award", we
          have a two-way tie.

Many students turn and stare towards Henry and Tom.

                    BRUNO (CONT'D)
          Henry Fitzpatrick and Tom Alexiou.

The crowd erupts in applause. Henry and Tom high five and jump on the stage to receive their mammoth BEER STEINS which they hold over their heads like a trophy.

                              CUT TO:

INT. LONDON AIRPORT - DAY

Henry lies hungover on Stephanie's lap in a row of waiting area seats. His mammoth beer stein lies near his carry-ons.

                    HENRY
          Oh my God!

Stephanie lovingly rubs his head for him.

                    STEPHANIE
          Poor baby.

Stephanie pats Henry's forehead rapid and hard. She thinks he's so cute. Henry sits up and pulls Stephanie close to him by the button on her shirt and passionately kisses her. Older couples look on and admire. Henry reaches in his jeans to adjust himself.

                    HENRY
          What's this?

                    STEPHANIE
          I'm not falling for that trick.

Henry pulls out some crumpled LIRA and holds it up to the light.

                              HENRY
                        (sighing)
               No more monopoly money. It's not enough
               to exchange.

30 feet away, RIVA (20) a slight Arab, and NEEDA (20) a well
built handsome Arab, intently observe Henry walking to an
insurance kiosk. Henry quickly fills out a slip, deposits
the money in an envelope and trots back to Stephanie.

                         ANNOUNCER (O.S.)
               Flight 181 non stop service to Seattle
               will be delayed one hour.

Henry stands with one arm clenched, marching.

                              HENRY
                        (singing ala the state
                         song)
               Washington, my home!

Stephanie pulls him toward her to kiss him, and to quiet him.

                            STEPHANIE
               You totally earned your award.

                              HENRY
               Thanks.

Riva and Needa observe them in love. Henry closes his eyes
and gets comfortable for a nap. Stephanie rests her head on
Henry's hip and closes her eyes.

INT. 747 - EARLY EVENING

Henry and Stephanie sit together in the rear of the airplane.
They wave at other young people taking their seats.

                            STEPHANIE
               Where's Adriane?

                              HENRY
               No telling.

                            STEPHANIE
               It's a little different than the way out
               here.

                              HENRY
               I'll say. You didn't want anything to do
               with me then.

Henry looks like a puppy dog forcing Stephanie to kiss him
again.

Time passes. The plane is airborne. Stephanie stirs from her nap on Henry's shoulder.

> PILOT (O.S.)
> (English Accent)
> ...On the right hand side are the lights of Lockerbie, and in the distance that's Glasgow. We invite you to sit back and enjoy the fl--.

> HENRY
> --or lay back and enjoy the fl--

Henry pushes the recline button on Stephanie's seat and lustfully kisses her. He reaches overhead without looking, turning off the OVER HEAD LIGHT BUTTON.

Just as he reaches the button, a deafening BOOM severs the plan in half. The rear of the aircraft remains intact and continues flying. The rear passengers see the front of the plane drift below them amid terrified SCREAMS and bodies being sucked into the black. Henry holds Stephanie tight.

> STEPHANIE
> What did you push?

> HENRY
> Nothing, I swear.

Henry huddles low in his seat with Stephanie, their faces pressed together as they realize their fate. They strain over the ferocious WIND.

Henry looks Stephanie dead in the eye and locks his arms around her like a vise. With his look, he somehow erases both of their fears.

> HENRY
> I love you.

Henry calmy but passionately kisses her.

SUPER: SPOKANE, WASHINGTON, NINE MONTHS EARLIER

An AERIAL VIEW of the pine-treed mountain city of Spokane.

EXT. TREE LINED STREET - SPOKANE - AFTERNOON

Henry dribbles his BASKETBALL past late-summer browned lawns wearing his GONZAGA basketball T-shirt. He jogs toward an active portable SPRINKLER in front of a white Craftsman style home and jumps through it.

He drives for a lay-up. SWOOSH, he makes it, but then
grimaces, stops and holds his throat as he slowly shakes his
head. He enters the rear kitchen door letting the screen
door BANG.

INT. KITCHEN

Henry plops his backpack on a round kitchen table in the
cheery middle class kitchen. On the counter, a small 12 INCH
TV plays a vintage OPRAH show. Henry spies an ENVELOPE
supported between a small flower vase and two cookies on a
plate. He rips open the envelope.

Henry's mother, ALICE (40) attractive and fit, but still a
bit of a hippy, waits in the wings for his reaction with her
arms crossed, grinning.

                    HENRY
          MOM!

Henry spins around to find her and hugs her tightly.

                    ALICE
          Dad would be so proud.

                    HENRY
          They were probably feeling sorry for me.

Alice holds Henry in front of her.

                    ALICE
          Oh fiddlesticks. You got that all on
          your own.

                    HENRY
          I can't leave you alone now.

                    ALICE
          You are going, buster. Your dad would
          have cut off his right leg to go on a
          trip like this.

                    HENRY
          That's about all they left of him.

                    ALICE
          I meant when he was your age. It was
          just about that time I met your father.

                    HENRY
          Really?

                    ALICE
          He was so immature when I met him, I
          hated him. But after a while I couldn't
          resist ol' Hank Fitzpatrick.

Alice grabs a FRAME off the counter and admires a beaming
family PICTURE of herself, Henry and his handsome father.

                    HENRY
          I hope I find someone as good as you.

Alice turns toward the small TV picturing a clean cut local
newscaster.

                    NEWSMAN (ON TV)
          No group has yet claimed responsibility
          for the bomb attack at Berlin's La Belle
          discotheque which killed two American
          servicemen and injured over 60.

                    ALICE
          You be careful. There are crazy people
          over there trying to kill Americans
          because they're jealous.

                    HENRY
          I'm sure it's a little more involved than
          that mom.

                    ALICE
          Promise me you won't go looking for
          trouble. No one is going to bail you out
          over there.

                    HENRY
          We usually don't go looking for discos
          filled with jarheads.

Alice shakes her head.

                    ALICE
          Your father used to be a jarhead.

Henry reaches behind Alice to grab a cookie and change the
subject.

                    HENRY
                (mouth full)
          Mmm. Good job mom.

Henry hugs her again. Alice touches his forehead.

                    ALICE
          You sure you're OK honey? You feel a
          little warm.

Henry pulls away.

                    HENRY
          Fine, fine, just a little tired.

                    ALICE
          One more thing.

                    HENRY
          What this time?

Alice reaches in between her recipe books and pulls out a
beautiful old leather writing JOURNAL.

                    ALICE
          It's still empty. Grama gave me this for
          my trip abroad, but, as you know,
          instead... We had you!

                    HENRY
          Good guilt trip mom.

Henry examines it.

                    HENRY
           This is rad.

                    ALICE
          Just a few line a day so I can see what
          you were up to.

Henry grabs the other cookie, toasts her with it and exits
the room, flipping through the journal.

INT. BATHROOM

Henry closes the door, goes to the mirror and pulls his eye
lids down and check his glands. He opens his mouth and peers
in.

EXTREME CLOSE UP of his trembling uvula.

                    HENRY
          Aaaaaahhhhhhh! Fuck.

Henry looks at a doctor's prescription that reads ACUTE
MONONUCLEOSIS, the words BED REST and LIQUIDS are apparent.
Henry exits.

INT. KITCHEN

Henry heads out the back door.

                    ALICE
          Where do you think you're going? You've
          got to pack.

                    HENRY
          Got to tell the gang!

EXT. BART'S HOUSE -DAY

BART WINSLOW (20), a 6'5" mountain stud wearing a cowboy hat
and tight jeans, sits on his front porch railing with Henry
and TABITHA STRONG(20) a buxom brunette who has no idea how
hot she is.

                    TABITHA
               (southern accent)
          Baby, how was I supposed to know I had
          that ma..mo..mononuclear digliceride--

                    HENRY
          --just call it Mono.

                    TABITHA
          I just thought I couldn't shake my
          hangover. We was just kissing...then.

                    HENRY
          Anything else to tell me?

                    TABITHA
          Just that I'll miss you a ton and I'll
          try to be good.

                    HENRY
          Don't be good for me.

                    BART
               (cowboy accent)
          You gonna get yourself a squaw over
          there?

                    HENRY
          They're called ragazzas.

                    BART
          Boy, you are so damn smart.

Bart socks Henry on the arm nearly sending him over the
railing.

> BART (CONT'D)
> How bout a Rain-dog for the road? Bet
> they won't have these over there.

Bart twists open a 16-ounce BOTTLE of RAINEER beer with his
teeth and expertly snaps the bottle CAP, sailing it directly
to a red painted BULL'S-EYE on the side of an old garage.
Thousands of bottle caps lie beneath in a pile.

> HENRY
> No thanks Bam-Bam. I just want to get
> better.

> BART
> Vitamin R is good for ya!

Bart swills the Raineer.

> BART (CONT'D)
> Here's to Henry! Go show them eye-talians
> why you left Cheyenne.

> HENRY
> I'm gonna miss you guys.

Henry holds out his arms. They hug tightly in a ring.

> HENRY (CONT'D)
> One, two, three---(in unison)Break!

They quickly release. Henry grabs a BEER anyway.

> HENRY (CONT'D)
> Doc did say plenty of liquids.

Henry twists the cap off and snaps his bottle cap. Bart
smiles, and nods "atta boy".

> HENRY (cont'd)
> Thanks a ton for the suitcase.

> BART
> I put your name on it and everything.

Henry tap kicks a brown canvas SUITCASE complete with
NAMETAG, air toasts Bart and winks. Bart opens another
Raineer with his teeth and sails the bottle cap toward the
red bull's eye.

A CLOSE UP of the whizzing bottle cap hits the red bull's eye
dead center. The EXTREME CLOSE UP of the red becomes a RED
EYE. As the picture widens, a marksman's target depicting
the familiar UNCLE SAME RECRUITING POSTER, "He Wants You"
appears. A bullet rips through the poster's eye.

EXT. SYRIAN DESERT - MORNING

SUPER: SOMEWHERE IN SYRIA

AL-BANRI (20) a young Arab, stands proudly after his bull's eye shot directly in to Uncle Sam's EYE. Several young Arabs, all dressed in well-worn military fatigues, congratulate and admire his skill. The next young Arab lines up to fire his rifle at the target. A CLOSE UP of the whizzing bullet hits Uncle Sam's other red eye. The eye turns from red to blue, and then to a REAL EYE.

MATCH CUT: Henry's eye.

INT. AIRPORT TERMINAL - SEATTLE - AFTERNOON

Henry blinks his EYE and looks at the airport monitors, suitcase by his side in the busy terminal. ADRIANE MOSHALINI (20), a perky dyed blond dressed provocatively in high heels, skips up to Henry with her carry-on and a mound of saran-wrapped BROWNIES.

> ADRIANE
> Sweetie! I'm so sorry about your pops.

Adriane motherly hugs Henry and attempts to kiss him but he turns away.

> HENRY
> I've got the Mono, Adriane. No kissing.

> ADRIANE
> That sucks. I had it too! It's like getting bit by the Tsetse fly.

> HENRY
> When have you been bitten by the Tsetse fly?

> ADRIANE
> Never, but it sounded exotic, like going to Florence! Can you fucking believe it?

Adriane grabs his arm.

> HENRY
> It is going to be sweet.

> ADRIANE
> Speaking of sweet, guess what I made us for the trip?

Adriane presents a large mound of brownies.

                    ADRIANE (CONT'D)
          These will make you forget you have Mono.
          There's like a hundred bucks of Oregon
          Sinse in here.

                    HENRY
          I can't.

                    ADRIANE
          I've already had two and believe me you
          can. I did it with the butter.

                    HENRY
          Doc said I gotta cool it until it's gone.

                    ADRIANE
          Dude, they are all natural, and it will
          make the trip a snap.

Henry flirts with the brownies.

                    ADRIANE
          You just gotta party through your illness
          babe.

                    HENRY
          Just give me the damn thing.

Adriane hands him one and plants a wet smooch on Henry.
Henry pulls back in shock that he's infected her.

                    ADRIANE
          Don't worry. You can't get Mono twice.

They amble towards the gate, arms slung on each other.

                    ADRIANE
          How's mom dealing?

INT. AIR CANADA AIRPLANE - EVENING

Now in flight, fifteen 20 year old students act their age
grouped together in rows.

PATRICK(20) an affable Irish-American jock, wearing an A's
baseball cap backwards, sits next to the now stoned Henry.
Patrick adds another empty beer can to his already filled
tray.

                    HENRY
          No more.

Henry pushes his beer onto Patrick's tray.

                        PATRICK
              Pussy!

Henry grabs an empty beer can to toast and abate Patrick. He
puts the can down and snuggles to the window.

A harried STEWARDESS struggles to keep up supplying beers to
the rowdy coeds.

Patrick grabs two cradled in her elbow, pops one open and
immediately downs it.

                        PATRICK
              Aaah. Can't believe you of all people
              passing up a free coldie. You've got to
              seize the moment. Isn't that what you
              said.

                        HENRY
              Seriously dude, this Mono is fucked.

                        PATRICK
              Put this on that swollen vagina of yours.

Patrick rams a beer in Henry's crotch. Henry finally gets
pissed and socks cowering Patrick in the arm, throwing the
can to the floor and snuggling back to the window.

                        PATRICK (CONT'D)
              Or hers, check out some of this kindness
              for our pleasure this year.

Henry cracks open his eyes. Just then MELODY (20) plump, but
bubbling with personality, struts by and smiles at Henry.

                        PATRICK
                   (softly)
              Not the fat chick dude.

Patrick points behind Melody to stunning Stephanie flicking
her hair coquettishly, talking to new friends. Henry's
interest is piqued. He stares at her as she sits back down
with showy Nella and NANCY (20), a prim and proper girl
dressed in a yellow monogrammed sweater with a gold add-a-
bead necklace.

                        PATRICK (CONT'D)
              I've never seen half of them.

                        HENRY
              Where is that one from?

Henry points to Stephanie. Patrick grabs his ORIENTATION
PAMPHLET and scans the pictures and bios.

                       PATRICK
Let's see. She's from Mt. Holypoke or
something. You can tell she's got bank.

                       HENRY
It's Holyoke dude.

Stephanie finally looks over at Henry. Their eyes lock.
This is it.

                       PATRICK
Some of these chicks are gonna need bank
statements before you pork 'em. Bet ya
none of them are on student loans like
us.

                       HENRY
Doesn't matter dude. They wanna get laid
and have fun too.

Stephanie stays smiling at Henry as Nella pulls her down
towards her.

                       PATRICK
But they are all gonna wanna fuck
Italians for their scrapbooks.

                       HENRY
Once they figure out they don't shower
and their Dicks aren't cut, they'll be
begging to get back in our good graces.

                       PATRICK
You're usually right dude.

Henry stretches his arms behind his head and smiles towards
Stephanie, confident that's he's irresistible.

Nella and Stephanie look at the roster, pointing at pictures
as they go.

                       NELLA
                    (to Stephanie)
Poor...

Nella points to another picture.

                       NELLA

Has an afro...

She points to the next.

                    NELLA
        Potentially jealous of me.

                    STEPHANIE
        What about him?

Stephanie points to Henry's picture.

                    NELLA
        Jennifer told me his dad just died...zero
        cash, don't waste your time.

Stephanie looks sweetly at the picture of Henry smiling.
Nella can see she's not convinced.

                    NELLA (CONT'D)
        And I heard he just got some sleeping
        disease or something you get from sex
        with sluts.

                    STEPHANIE
        It's just mono--

                    NELLA
        --We are not hanging out with the boys
        from the trailer park. Once you dip that
        low, none of the right boys will touch
        you.

Stephanie rolls her eyes and starts looking in a fashion
magazine to change the subject. Nella sticks her finger
right in her magazine on an AD.

                    NELLA (CONT'D)
        Ferra-fucking-gamo...we are going to be
        right there!

She jerks the magazine from Stephanie.

                    STEPHANIE
        Maybe he has enough cash for you.

                    NELLA
        Oldies with stinky breath and grey pubies
        are forbidden also, ewwwwh.

                    STEPHANIE
        Been there, huh?

                    NELLA
        I think he's dead anyway. However,
        silver foxes are another subject.

Nella looks at the magazine seeming to imagine herself with Ferragamo. Stephanie turns and smiles over her shoulder to Henry watching him get comfortable.

> PATRICK
> One more dude, the even number rule, you
> can't just have 5.

Drunk Patrick nudges Henry who is now passed out leaning against the window. Just before Patrick speaks again, Melody approaches the boys from behind ready to share her family-size package of OREOS. Patrick is unaware Melody is right behind him.

> PATRICK
> Dude, do you know what fat chicks and
> mopeds have in common?

Henry is passed out. Patrick bumps him with his elbow.

> PATRICK
> They're fun to ride until someone sees
> you on one. Get it?

Henry nods in delirium. Melody looks down, completely sad and slowly turns around to her seat.

Stephanie slowly approaches Patrick and Henry hoping to meet Henry.

> PATRICK (CONT'D)
> Hey aren't you the girl from Mt.
> Holypoke?--

> STEPHANIE
> --very funny--

> PATRICK
> --my buddy here think's you're cute.

Stephanie stands up straight. Patrick nudges Henry's cadaver. Stephanie is mildly offended he won't respond.

> PATRICK (CONT'D)
> Don't ya, Henry? Hey!

Patrick jolts Henry. Henry appears to be looking right at Stephanie through slits in his eyes, even though he's fast asleep.

> HENRY
> Fuck off!

Stephanie is startled and starts to leave.

PATRICK
(to Stephanie)
You are gonna love him, he's huge.

Patrick spreads his hands a foot apart. Stephanie scurries
away. Patrick hits motionless Henry.

PATRICK (CONT'D)
Dude, you owe me big, man. I always give
you the hook up.

EXT. SYRIAN DESERT - MORNING

SUPER: SOMEWHERE IN SYRIA

Cheap SHOES run single file on parched dirt and stop in front
of a sweltering sunglassed Arab instructor holding a
clipboard. ABU (40), barks at several young recruits,
including Riva and Needa, boarding a weathered open-aired
Army truck.

ABU
(yelling)
Freedom Fighters! Prepare to regain your
homeland!

Abu jumps on the truck. It abruptly takes off in a cloud of
dust.

INT. FRANKFURT AIRPORT - MORNING

Henry and Patrick stumble off the plane and follow the crowd.

PATRICK
(singing)
I'm free...to do what I want...any--

HENRY
--My throat's fuckin' killing me.

Henry grimaces as he swallows.

PATRICK
Sorry I made you party dude.

Patrick goes to help out Henry with his bag.

HENRY
That's OK, I'm a big boy.

PATRICK
That's what you keep saying.

> HENRY
> Yeah? Your mom told me I almost split her
> in half.

Henry and Patrick laugh and head toward the agitated director
of the program, PADRE VIA, a 60 year-old portly, balding and
serious Jesuit.

> PADRE VIA
> Two more drunks to add to the roster.
> Names?

> HENRY
> Fitzpatrick.

> PATRICK
> Flaherty.

Padre Via checks off their names.

> PADRE VIA
> What are you staring at? Get on the bus!

Henry and Patrick meekly obey.

> PATRICK
> Wow, he's cranky pants.

They continue past Bruno who stands greeting only girls as
they walk by.

> BRUNO
> Ladies...ladies.

> PATRICK
> And he, is totally after box.

Bruno hears Patrick. He looks up and smiles at them. They
nod back.

> BRUNO
> Gentleman.

INT. HOTEL LOBBY - MAINZ,GERMANY - AFTERNOON

Henry and Patrick enter the shabby lobby with their years
worth of luggage amid bustling students and their gear.
Henry spies Tom dressed in checkered VANS and surf shorts.

> TOM
> "On-Ray" what the fuck is up? Were you
> dieing in Slo-kan this summer?

                    HENRY
          Actually had so much fun I got Mono.

Henry opens his mouth to prove it. Tom peers in.

                    TOM
          Oooh, nasty dude...had it. Best thing to
          do is party thr--

                    HENRY
          Yeah, I know. Been doing that.
          Seriously dude, I am wrecked.

                    TOM
          Looks like someone needs to smoke some
          pot.

                    HENRY
          Not.

                    TOM
          Dude, think of it as fun chemo for your
          mono.

Henry's eyes dart sadly to the ground. Tom notices, but
inadvertenly digs a bigger hole.

                    TOM (CONT'D)
          I mean, you don't wanna make things easy
          for the virus--

                    HENRY
          --I get it. What the fuck are you doing
          smuggling pot here anyway?

                    TOM
          It's local.

                    HENRY
          So it probably has PCP or some surprise
          in it.

                    TOM
          Dude, that shit costs extra. You think
          they give it away?

Tom's eyes light up.

                    TOM (CONT'D)
          I know, you pussy!

Tom hums "Tequila" and does the Pee Wee Herman Tequila dance
before Henry interrupts.

                    HENRY
          Forget it dude. I'm getting better.

                    TOM
          You're going! We're on this trip once in
          our fucking lives.

                    HENRY
          But--

                    TOM
          So when you're 80 you're gonna say,
          "Damn, I'm glad I was a goody-goody
          bitch."

                    HENRY
          I might.

                    TOM
          But you're not, cause you're going...
          TEQUILA!

Tom pushes Henry out the front door of the Hotel.

INT. DARK GERMAN BAR -EVENING

Tom and Henry stroll in like studs. Kate sits alone at the
bar dressed in a leather motorcycle coat. Kate catches
Henry's eye and makes a BLOW-JOB MOTION to him with the beer
bottle she is slurping. Henry looks a bit scared and darts
his eyes for an empty spot away from her. Tom bounces
obliviously towards Kate, Henry must follow.

                    TOM
                (to bartender)
          Svei Tequila shots bitte.

                    HENRY
          You're so good.

Tom hands Henry his shot.

                    TOM
          Here's to the hole that never heals. The
          more you rub it the better it feels.

They CLINK glasses.

Tom shoots his first. While Tom's eyes are closed and
wincing, Henry throws his over his shoulder, dousing Kate's
curly mane.

                    KATE
          Hey!

Henry spins around, leans over and puts his arm around Kate pretending he knows her. She tussles the wet spot on her hair.

                    HENRY
               (whispering to Kate)
     Sorry.

                    HENRY (CONT'D)
           (to Tom)
     Hey, this is my good friend...

                    KATE
     Kate.

                    HENRY
     She loves Tequila shots.

Kate looks quizzically at Henry but plays along.

                    TOM
     Ya want one?

                    KATE
     Why not. It's going to be a long year
     with these simps.

Kate nods over toward a group of clean-cut Gonzaga girls dressed in college sweatshirts and headbands. Nella looks over and glares at Henry, quickly ignoring him.

Henry pretends to go to the bathroom, but heads out the front door, looking back at his ingenious introduction.

Tom and Kate knock back their shots and look into each others eyes. It's love at first sight.

INT. HOTEL ROOM - EVENING

Henry sits on the bed writing in his mother's journal.

                    HENRY (V.O.)
     ...and after Germany is Israel and then
     Turkey. Everyone is really cool,
     especially this one named Stephanie.
     More on her later.

Henry closes the journal and rolls over on his back, unzipping his fly, smiling, closing his eyes.

HENRY'S FANTASY:

Henry is on the plane locking eyes with Stephanie. (Suggest
Psychedelic Furs, "Love my Way") He motions her over with
his eyes to the empty seat next to him as he unzips his fly.
She eagerly vamps over to him and gazes down to see his
package. He is fast asleep, head cocked to one side, mouth
open.

END FANTASY

On the bed, Henry starts to drool from his wide-open MOUTH
with his hand still on his zipper.

INT. TERRORIST'S CLASSROOM - SYRIA - AFTERNOON

CLOSE UP: An open mouth.

The mouth belongs to an Arab recruit sleeping while Abu barks
orders in front of the full classroom.

Abu slaps the sleeping man on the shoulder.

                    ABU
          ...there were many careless mistakes at
          the discotheque.

Needa kicks Riva's chair. Riva turns around slightly but
looks forward again to avoid the wrath of Abu.

                    ABU
               (in Arabic)
          You have been chosen from your comrades
          because of your English.

Abu kicks Needa's chair again for his attention.

                    ABU (CONT'D)
               (in English)
          Most of your parents were murdered by
          them. Their land and farms stolen from
          them. Do not forget why you are here!
          The Israelis could not survive alone. It
          is only with their help that this
          slaughter occurred.

Abu slaps his pointer stick on a hanging MAP OF THE UNITED
STATES with RED PINS stuck in various cities.

                    ABU (CONT'D)
          Al-Banri, come here.

Al-Banri strides up to Abu.

                        ABU (CONT'D)
          You will be the first to represent your
          class with your Jewish looks. We have
          special assignment for you working in Tel-
          Aviv. You will not disappoint us!

Abu sternly grabs his shoulder! Al-Banri shakes his head in
assurance.

                        AL-BANRI
          For our People!

Al-Banri raises his fist.

The entire class CHEERS except for expressionless Needa
staring straight ahead.

EXT. OCTOBERFEST - DAY

SCREAMS of joy echo throughout the park. Patrick's FACE is
filled with glee as he rides the ROLLERCOASTER with Henry and
Tom. Their arms are raised.

The boys exit the ride. Patrick vigorously rubs Henry's
shoulders as he begs for them to slow down. Henry opens his
mouth to Tom for a check up.

                        TOM
          Your throat still looks like a hooker's
          vadge, but you're gonna be fine.

They continue past acres of amusement park rides and canopied
beer tents, with names like HOFBRAUHAUS. They spy Stephanie,
Nella and her gang ambling in to the AUSTRALIAN/NEW ZEALAND
tent. Henry's interest is piqued now.

                        HENRY
          In here!

                        PATRICK
          That's my boy.

They follow the girls into the beer tent.

INT. AUSTRALIAN/NEW ZEALAND BEER TENT

The tent overflows with drunks sitting at giant picnic tables
in continuous taunts. A large group performs the CHICKEN
DANCE on stage.

                        CROWD (LEFT SIDE)
          AUSSIE!!!!!

CROWD (RIGHT SIDE) (CONT'D)
KIWI!!!!

Nella finds a nearly empty table and begins to sit down until
she realizes Henry and company are right on her heels. She
gleefully spies a handsome blond YOUNG AUSSIE with his
friends and motions her crowd to sit with them at their
nearly full table. Henry is not dismayed and continues to
her table to crowd them in. Stephanie sits quietly mashed to
the end, and shyly smiles at Henry. Henry flirts back.

                    PATRICK
          Hey Nella, what up?

Patrick smiles knowing he's throwing a wrench in her plan to
get laid.

                    NELLA
          Nothing, we just met these really great
          guys here.

Nella puts her back to Patrick and looks only at her Aussie
who is completely hammered and smiling cock-eyed.

                    PATRICK
          He looks like a real talker!

The Aussie's friends give Patrick a "what's up" nod.

A St. Pauli Girl looking waitress loaded with beer steins
arrives. Nella hands her a wad of money and buys everyone
but Henry and company a round.

                    NELLA
               (to Aussie yelling)
          You getting pretty wasted?!

Nella leans in and tussles his chest. The Aussie wants to
answer, looking dead-on at her face, but instead PUKES on her
with firehose force. Nella is stunned at what her new beau
has done and seems almost anxious to forgive him when he gets
her square in the face again! All the boys ROAR with
laughter as Nella pulls a pretzel chunk out of her hair.

The Aussie smiles at the boys, proud of the laugh he produced
and takes another gulp of beer.

Patrick plucks a chunk out of Nella's hair and hurls it at
Tom. Tom takes his full STEIN and drenches Patrick also
hitting Henry. Henry takes his stein and drenches the other
side of the table including Stephanie. A massive BEER FIGHT
ensues, eventually infecting the entire pavilion in utterly
wonderful beer-fighting mayhem.

EXT. DACHAU CONCENTRATION CAMP - MORNING

The Gonzaginis mill near the entrance of Dachau, the international monument to what's left of the WWII Jewish concentration camp. All are woefully hungover hiding behind their sunglasses.

                    PADRE VIA
          Please show respect for what has gone on
          here.

                    TOM
                (to Henry and Patrick)
          What went on here? Except some bad
          architecture.

Padre Via glares at Tom.

                    PATRICK
          Dude, check it out.

Patrick points to a INFORMATION PLACARD depicting the timeline and some grisly scenes.

                    TOM
          No way man, I thought Via was kidding so
          I'd pay attention. Where was Uncle Sam
          to stop it?

                    HENRY
          Dude. You never heard of the Holocaust?

                    TOM
          Yeah, they're some metal band from Chino.

Patrick continues to be spellbound by the placard.

Tom, Patrick and Henry mill around in disbelief.

                    PATRICK
          You've definitely heard of Hitler,
          right?.

Patrick points to another large picture placard of Hitler, and also one with dead bodies piled on each other.

                    TOM
          Well, yeah dude. But all I remember was
          he had a really bad haircut and one ball.

                    HENRY
          It makes you so sad, no wonder we don't
          think about this stuff.

                    PATRICK
          You're starting to sound like a chick.

                    TOM
          He's right. I mean, who gives a shit
          where you nurse your hangover on Sunday
          morning. Guess he was afraid they might
          get all the sale items at the mall before
          he did.

                    PATRICK
          Man.

Patrick moves away.

                    PATRICK
          I don't wanna be around you when the
          lightning bolt hits.

                    TOM
          Dude, I'm not prejudice. I think Jewish
          chicks are hot.

Tom puts his finger in the air, pretending he's touching
something hot.

                    TOM
          ...and they always seem to have nice tits
          and dad's credit card right when the
          munchies ensue.

                    HENRY
          What trips me out is that he got other
          people to do it!

Tom jumps up and down with his arm raised.

                    TOM
          (a la Beastie Boys)That's why you gotta
          FIGHT!.. FOR YOUR RIGHT!....to PARRRRTY!

Padre Via glares at Tom. Henry hits Tom who abruptly quits.

                    HENRY
          We live some sheltered-ass lives.

                    PATRICK
          Why do you think everyone wants to move
          to the states?

                    TOM
               (matter of factly)
          For the waves and babes dude.

The boys start back to the bus.

> HENRY
> There's a lot more to America than
> California, Tom.

> TOM
> You mean the fly over zone?

> HENRY
> Yeah, that part.

The students shuffle back to the bus. Padre Via stands arms crossed.

> TOM
> Nice move Padre, taking us to that place
> fully hung-over.

> PADRE VIA
> Don't think it wasn't intentional. You
> candy-assed kids have to learn about the
> real world sometime.

> TOM
> Padre, You're a priest. You know you're
> not allowed to talk like that.

Tom is impressed by his language.

> PADRE VIA (CONT'D)
> Load em up!

Tom and gang silently enter the bus, beaten.

INT. TENT - SYRIA - NIGHT

By candle light, exhausted Riva sits upright on his cot and looks at a worn FAMILY PICTURE. He buries his head in his hand and wipes the tears from his eyes.

SERIES OF SHOTS:

DEAD SEA - The Gonzaginis joke and float around effortlessly in the aqua marine water.

TEL AVIV - Adriane has her picture taken next to a young soldier, touching his gun as if it were his manhood.

JERUSALEM - Students mill around the ancient city and ponder the wailing wall. They are stymied by the several people stuffing messages in its cracks. Gun toting SOLDIERS are everywhere.

INT. BAR - JERUSALEM - EVENING

The Gonzaginis party hard, ordering shots and beers galore.
Stephanie enters the bathroom. Henry follows after her to
wait for her moment alone with Henry..

Melody tromps up holding a Long Island Iced Tea. She is
obviously drunk.

>   MELODY
>   Henry Fitzpatrick.

>   HENRY
>   Hey, what's up?

Henry shakes her hand.

>   MELODY
>   I just wanted to say, ever since first
>   year Italian I've always thought you were
>   the cutest--

Melody rams her tongue down Henry's throat. Henry is trapped
and freaked. The bathroom door opens. Stephanie smirks
right into Henry's wide eyes while she molests him.

>   STEPHANIE
>   Pardon me. Don't want to interrupt
>   anything.

Henry holds his finger up to Stephanie to wait while lip
locked, but she just walks away.

INT. HOTEL ROOM - DAYBREAK

Tom and Henry sit in their disheveled room with Kate, still
naked under Tom's covers. Tom hops out of bed.

>   TOM
>   Dude, where's plumpy?

Henry covers his head with a pillow.

>   HENRY
>   And right in front of Stephanie. I'm
>   screwed. She must think I'll bang
>   anything.

>   KATE
>   You do.

>   HENRY
>   But she can't know that. Steph's so hot.

                         TOM
          Did I show you, 14 bucks!

Tom presents a golf ball size chunk of HASH.

                         HENRY
          Dude, in two hours we're on super-agro
          Hell-All Airlines going to Turkey.
          You're gonna get corn holed in jail like
          on "Midnight Express".

Henry tosses Tom face down on the bed and pretends to hump
him. Tom looks around from the bed.

                         TOM
          Fuck man, you're right.

Shortly thereafter.

Tom, Henry, Kate and Adriane take turns smoking hash out of a
toilet paper roll pipe sitting on the bed. Adriane finishes
her turn, COUGHS, and hands the pipe to Tom.

                         ADRIANE
          My God! That's harsh.

                         TOM
          Waste not, want not.

Tom takes a big hit. Henry gets in front of Tom and draws an
"air" rectangle with opposing fingers. Tom tries to follow
his fingers and gets confused.

                         HENRY
          You are SO not "OK" to fly.

INT. TEL AVIV AIRPORT- BEHIND COUNTER -9:15 AM

Al-Banri loads bags onto the conveyor belt and nervously
looks around, darting his eyes to a BLUE CANVAS BAG near his
feet.

INT. TEL AVIV AIRPORT -LOBBY

Armed guards patrol the terminal. The Gonzaginis line up for
El AL Airlines' rigorous open bag check and battery of
questions. Vuarnet and Walkman clad Henry and Tom hang out
grooving in the back of the line. Henry smiles to Stephanie
who stands with Nella. Nella turns Stephanie away from him
matter of factly.

                         NELLA
          You'll be working graveyard at Denny's to
          buy pot for their bongs.

Patrick overhears her and gets annoyed. Stephanie rolls her
eyes at Nella who fixes her tightly bunned hair.

                    NELLA (CONT'D)
          My head is killing me! This is like
          soooo inconvenient.

                    STEPHANIE
          My god, loosen that thing.

Stephanie loosens Nella's hair band. She is instantly
relaxed.

                    NELLA
          This high security would never fly in the
          states.

                    STEPHANIE
          Guess it's better than getting blown up.

                    PATRICK
          But not better than getting blown.

                    NELLA
          You wonder why you don't have a date.

Patrick waggles his tongue at Nella through a "V" he forms
with his fingers. Henry kicks Patrick in the butt to get him
to stop and smiles at Stephanie to show her his matureness.

Henry continues to groove. (Suggest the Cure, "Let's go to
Bed",) as the lyric "Let me take your hand I'm shaking like
Milk" is sung, a well-built SECURITY GUARD (30), approaches
Henry and taps him on the shoulder. Tom notices first.

                    TOM
                (to Henry)
          Dude, he knows you're stoned.

Henry is paranoid for a split second until he sees Tom
snicker.

                    SECURITY GUARD
          Scuse please.

                    HENRY
          Yeah?

Henry removes his earphones.

                    SECURITY GUARD
          May I speak with you for a minute.

                    HENRY
        Sure?

The guard motions Henry to follow him. Henry looks at Tom.
Tom mouths "busted" and snickers again. They walk side by
side through a door marked "NO ADMITTANCE".

INT. SECURITY OFFICE

                    HENRY
        I'm totally fine. Since when is it a
        crime to be a little loose---

The guard walks over to a REUTERS NEWS TELETYPE MACHINE
ticking away and rips off the latest TELETYPE story and hands
it to Henry. The machine continues loudly TYPING.

                    HENRY
        What's this?

                    SECURITY GUARD
        The Abu-Nidal terrorist group attacked
        our check-in gates in Rome and Vienna
        thirty minutes ago.

(An actual event)

                    HENRY
        Holy shit?! Was anyone killed?

                    SECURITY GUARD
        Eighteen of you Americans. We have word
        they will try to attack us today.

                    HENRY
        Like this?

Henry points to the teletype scared.

                    SECURITY GUARD
        We have too much firepower here. Probably
        their cowardly way, with a bomb.

                    HENRY
        A bomb? Did you say bomb?

Henry tosses the paper on the floor.

                    SECURITY GUARD
        Not if you help me stop them.

                    HENRY
        Dude. You gotta get somebody else.

                    SECURITY GUARD
          I picked you. You have honest face,
          like...like Richie Cunningham.

                    HENRY
          Seriously dude, there are plenty of folks
          out there that are so wholesome you could
          grow a plant on them.

Henry wrings his face in his hands.

                    SECURITY GUARD
          I need you.

                    HENRY
          I mean, what can "I" do? I don't even
          know how to shoot a gun.

                    SECURITY GUARD
          Help me test our security. We believe
          someone on our staff is with their cause.
          This will be the excuse we need to shut
          the flight down and re-check the bags.

The guard produces a BIBLE with its innards removed
containing a diffused bomb.

                    HENRY
          How do I know you aren't in on it and
          that thing is for real?

                    SECURITY GUARD
          You can see the cut wires. You must
          trust me. You can tell no one.

                    HENRY
          So, I just walk up to the guy, he finds
          it and I get arrested. That sounds
          great! Are you nuts?

                    SECURITY GUARD
          I will be right there. I will tell you
          exactly what to say, just look confused.

                    HENRY
          That part's easy.

                    SECURITY GUARD
          You will be saving the lives of all your
          friends!

                    HENRY
          OK. I'll do it!

The guard explains more to Henry as he puts the BIBLE in a WHITE GIFT SHOP BAG and place it inside his suitcase.

INT. TEL AVIV AIRPORT - LOBBY

                    HENRY
          Forgot this.

Henry shows his PASSPORT to Tom and glances over to the guard and assures him he won't spill the beans. The guard nods.

INT. TEL AVIV AIRPORT - BEHIND COUNTER

Al-Banri anxiously loads bags on the conveyor belt after they have been checked and given a GREEN STICKER. The BLUE CANVAS BAG with a green sticker sits ominously to his right.

X-RAY VISION allows us to see the bomb ticking inside for a split-second. Al-Banri nervously looks over at the bag and gazes out at the rows of check-in passengers.

INT. TEL AVIV AIRPORT - LOBBY

Henry advances in the bag check line. He approaches the twenty something young lady CHECKER with his tan canvas SUITCASE.

                    CHECKER
               (accent)
          Open please.

Henry complies. She routinely checks his belongings.

                    CHECKER (CONT'D)
          Did you leave your bag unattended?

                    HENRY
          No, well, kinda. When I came out of the
          bathroom, my friends weren't there,
          but...nah.

                    CHECKER
          Does anything look different?

Henry scans the bag, trying not to look at the white plastic gift shop bag.

INT. TEL AVIV AIRPORT - BEHIND COUNTER

Al-Banri carefully puts the BLUE canvas BAG with the bomb on the conveyor belt headed towards the plane.

INT. TEL AVIV AIRPORT -LOBBY

The checker grabs the plastic bag; takes out the Bible; opens
it up and nearly faints as she quickly sounds the loud
bullhorn ALARM.

INT. TEL AVIV AIRPORT - BEHIND COUNTER

Al-Banri panics. His eyes dart around as he immediately
grabs the bomb off the belt putting it back in its original
spot. Guards come running towards Henry, guns drawn.

INT. TEL AVIV AIRPORT - LOBBY

Henry's eyes are as wide as saucers. He has been scared out
of being stoned.

                    ATTENDING GUARD
          What has happened here?!

The original security guard cruises up with a broad smile.

                    SECURITY GUARD
          Making sure everyone is safe. Shut down
          the plane and re-check everything!

INT. TEL AVIV AIRPORT BEHIND COUNTER

Al-Banri seethes. He burns a glance at Henry who he
recognizes is the cause of the alarm.

FANTASY - DARK OFFICE

Al-Banri stands blindfolded, hands bound in a dark room with
a single light bulb. A gun is held to his head by Abu. The
gun FIRES.

END FANTASY

Al-Banri sees the guards and Henry now joking and shaking
hands. Al-Banri must know his name! The checker places a
GREEN STICKER on Henry's suitcase and tosses it on the
conveyor belt headed towards Al-Banri. As the suitcase
passes sweaty Al-Banri, he looks at Henry and rips the
baggage tag off.

IT READS:

                    HENRY FITZPATRICK

                    1364 SHARP AVENUUE

                    SPOKANE, WASHINGTON

Al-Banri glares at Henry merrily explaining his antics to Tom and friends while walking down the final hallway to the plane. Padre Via argues with the security guard.

INT. HOTEL MAR MAR - INSTANBUL - AFTERNOON

Students ride the golden escalators to the lobby of the luxury Etap Mar Mar Hotel.

> TOM
> (to Henry a la Mission
> Impossible)
> Da da da da da da duh duh duh--

> HENRY
> That's right. You owe me *huge* dude.

> KATE
> I'm sure you saved our lives.

Kate pats Henry on the back as they walk towards their bags in a pile. Henry kicks aside a stack of HERALD newspapers next to the pile. The headline reads: ABU-NIDAL ATTACK ON ROME AND VIENNA KILLS 18.

INT. ABU'S OFFICE - NIGHT

Abu talks on the phone in front of a dated computer with the same copy of the HERALD.

> ABU
> You are a failure and will be punished!

INT. AL-BANRI'S APARTMENT - NIGHT

> AL-BANRI
> It is not my fault. He is the one.

Al-Banri stares at the luggage tag.

INTERCUT AS NEEDED

Abu punches they keys of his computer. Henry's FATHER appears on the computer with FITZPATRICK CIA printed near the side.

> ABU
> But you say he is young?

> AL-BANRI
> Yes, near my age.

                    ABU
          Well, many people say I look very young
          too.

Abu puts his side to the mirror and sucks in his gut putting
his hand on his belly.

                    ABU (CONT'D)
          I have two perfect ones to take care of
          this assignment.

                    AL-BANRI
          But I must finish it!

Abu pulls out two FILES. They are RIVA and NEEDA'S.

Al-Banri scans the MAP of the U.S. He finds SPOKANE and
circles it with a red felt tip pen.

                    ABU
          You had your chance to be a hero. First
          we will threaten the French with a bomb
          scare to raise more money first.

                    AL-BANRI (O.S.)
          But I found him.

Abu ignores him and hangs up.

EXT. ROME AIRPORT - DAY

Padre Via checks off students names as they enter the bus.
Tom and Henry remain inside clicking last minute pictures of
the mayhem and bullet holes from the terrorist shootout.

                    PADRE VIA
          Fitzpatrick!

Henry's ears perk up. He heads out the door.

                    HENRY
          We had a burger right--

                    PADRE VIA
          Save it. You kids are really sick
          sometimes.

Tom shoots Padre Via a peace sign and says nothing.

INT. TOUR BUS - DAY

Students lounge in various creative positions on the bus
seats. Tom rests his head on Kate's shoulder as she rocks out
to blaring HEAVY METAL MUSIC on her Walkman.

Henry sits alone writing in his journal. His foot is pushed
through to the next seat where Adriane, dressed in Turkish
Belly Dancer garb, expertly massages his socked foot.

Henry admires Stephanie talking near Nella. Stephanie turns
around to find Henry staring. She seems a bit annoyed that
he's being worshipped by Adriane. Nella jerks Stephanie
shirt.

Time passes.

The bus is now on the city streets of Florence passing an
inordinate amount of uncomfortable sweaty Italians, trash and
Vespas spewing black smoke.

                    TOM
          No Way! We're spending a year in this
          dump! This is like Gardena.

                    NANCY
          Now Tom, look at their great style and
          culture.

Nancy smiles out the window observing a hip couple and then
to a large woman in a moo-moo wearing sandals, waddling
slowly. The woman stops and opens a large woven purse to
grab a bandana. She first wipes her brow and then, without
warning, her hand disappears under her moo-moo for a wipe of
her nether regions where she tosses the bandana back in her
purse. Nancy quickly covers her eyes with both hands like a
child.

                    PATRICK
          And the trash...the pollution...the dog
          shit.

Patrick and Tom look dumbfounded out the window at people
expertly dodging a pile of dog poo. Nancy tries to stay
positive.

                    NANCY
          Look at the history, the beautiful
          buildings!

                    TOM
          Look, that's the same arch my dad built
          for the Riveria models in Irvine.

                    NANCY
          I think that arch beat your dad's by a
          few hundred years, silly.

The bus approaches Piazzale Michelangelo with its spectacular
view of the city.

The Gonzaginis exit and line up on the stairs with the DUOMO
in the background at the direction of Bruno. It is hotter
than hell and humid. Some guys immediately take off their
shirts. Nancy maintains her outfit sweating profusely,
shoulders slumped, holding her wooden handled purse. Her
composure is her duty.

EXT. PIAZZALE MICHELANGELO

                    BRUNO
          Line up! The quicker we get this over
          with, the quicker we check you into your
          pensione, the quicker you go drink beer.

                    PADRE VIA
          They don't need any encouragement.

                    BRUNO
          It's better than saying get drunk and
          laid.

Padre Via throws up his arms and walks towards the students.
He argues with a couple shirtless boys to put their shirts
back. They just move away from him. Everyone is finally
lined up. The city looms in the background.

                    PHOTOGRAPHER
               (thick accent)
          Everyone say Amore!

                    GROUP
          Amore!

The shirtless boys flex their muscles.

The photographer snaps the photo. The photo freezes and a
border appears around the picture. A CURSIVE "Gonzaga a
Firenze 87-88" appears letter by letter at the bottom.

EXT. SYRIAN DESERT - AFTERNOON

Twenty young unsmiling Arabs line up in rows waiting for
their picture to be taken. A photographer focuses under a
black cloak next to his almost antique CAMERA. The
photographer pulls his head out from under his cloak.

                    PHOTOGRAPHER
               (in Arabic)
          Everyone say Allah Akbar!

                    GROUP
          Allah Akbar.

INT. PENSIONE BELLETINI - FLORENCE - AFTERNOON

Pensione Belletini is a 300-year-old beautiful original
Palazzo with tiled floors and leather couches, located in the
center of Florence.

Students file up the stairs and head down the hall past Bruno
directing them to their rooms.

> BRUNO
> More roommates, more room, no whining.
> Mommy's not here.

Henry and Patrick hobble down the corridor with their
luggage. They glance at Nancy sitting on one of her many
suitcases weeping.

> HENRY
> Hey Nance, what's the matter?

> NANCY
> (sobbing)
> Ohhh, Henry, I know you're going to tease
> me.

> HENRY
> Try me.

> NANCY
> I needed a single. But I just can't live
> in...in...this. There's no closet space.
> The bathroom has one of the ga..gab--

> PATRICK
> Gabinettos. Shit holes in the ground.
> You've never had to aim before?

> HENRY
> Why do you think Italian women have such
> great thighs?

> NANCY
> I've never thought of that.

Nancy perks up, wipes the tears from her eyes and squeezes
her thigh. Patrick goes in to her bathroom and starts to pee
loudly.

> NANCY (CONT'D)
> Thanks Henry, I've got a lot of adjusting
> to do.

                    PATRICK
                 (still peeing)
          Shitting in a hole in the ground is the
          least of our problems. There's no
          McDonald's OR Burger Ki--

                    HENRY
          But there are plenty of bars, no drinking
          age, and the kid is almost back to 100%!

Henry feels his glands. Patrick shakes off in the bathroom to
the mild horror, yet intrigue of Nancy.

                    PATRICK
          See ya.

Patrick and Henry continue down the hall.

                    HENRY
          She has a nice rack under that sweater.
          You should get on that.

                    PATRICK
          Too much work. No one is seeing that
          except her doctor.

They kick the door open to their stark room. Patrick goes
directly to the toilet.

                    PATRICK (CONT'D)
          Didn't want to be rude and drop my log at
          Nancy's.

                    HENRY
          You're so thoughtful. Turn the fucking
          fan on.

Patrick pokes his head out from the bathroom.

                    PATRICK
          We're lucky to have a lightbulb.

                    HENRY
          Ugggh.

EXT. ABU'S OFFICE - AFTERNOON

A single LIGHTBULB illuminates the run-down office.

                    ABU
          I have special assignment for you.

Abu hands Needa and Riva plane tickets and new passports.

ABU
You are both going to America.

Riva raises his arm.

RIVA
For our people!

Abu walks away. Needa rolls his eyes at Riva.

NEEDA
You are such a hole licker. You say it
like you don't even mean it.

Needa makes a closed "OK" sign and puts his tongue in it.

RIVA
We are going aren't we?

Needa mildly nods and checks out his fake PASSPORT and
TICKET.

INT. PALAZZO ANTINORI - HALLWAY - DAY

Students mill around looking at their class schedules and
talking in the large hallway of the 600-year old Palazzo that
serves as their school. The bell RINGS.

Henry notices Stephanie walking with Nella. He waves.
Stephanie returns a small wave and a smile. Stephanie enters
the classroom first. Henry follows on her heels.

INT. CLASSROOM

Stephanie sits down. There is an empty seat next to her.
Nella jumps up from her seat to take the empty seat, thus
thwarting Henry. She flashes him a smug grin. Henry sits
next to Nella to drive her crazy.

MRS.BALDINI,(65) a frail Italian teacher with dyed dark brown
hair wearing a cashmere sweater, stands at the front of the
classroom.

MRS. BALDINI
(in Italian only)
Attention students, as you know a
condition of your acceptance into our
program was a minimum of one year of
Italian. If you don't understand me it's
going to be a long year.

Mrs. Baldini strolls around the classroom.

> MRS. BALDINI (CONT'D)
> Does everyone understand me?

Most of the students nod. Nella realizes everyone is
nodding. Nella begins to nod. Mrs. Baldini strides up to
Nella and plays with her hair.

> MRS. BALDINI (CONT'D)
> Bella donna, you don't understand a word
> I'm saying, do you my little dumb bunny?

Henry, Stephanie and a few others who understand chuckle.
Nella nervously nods and smiles looking around at the
laughter.

> MRS. BALDINI (CONT'D)
> This class isn't going to be a joke like
> back in the states. I am not afraid to
> give F's, so let's start with a quiz.

Mrs. Baldini passes out a quiz. Many students are befuddled,
including Nella who darts her eyes around to see whose paper
is in view. Henry effortlessly begins his quiz and smirks at
Nella trying to look at his paper. He teases her, hiding the
answers and then showing her. Nella is hypnotized like a
rabbit and a snake straining to see his answers.

Stephanie smiles at what is going on while easily whipping
through her quiz.

Mrs. Baldini walks up, grabs Nella's quiz and RIPS it up!

> MRS. BALDINI (CONT'D)
> (still in Italian)
> Smiling and your father's money might
> work in America.

Henry makes an "ooooooh" face at furious Nella. Stephanie
smiles with her eyes only at Henry to stay loyal to Nella.

The Bell RINGS. Students hand in their quizzes and disperse.
Nella is furious.

> NELLA
> Henry, you think you're so fucking smart.

> HENRY
> Moi? Come on now baby, it's easier to
> love me than fight me.

> NELLA
> Fuck you. You're history in my group of
> friends.

Nella storms down the stairs. Patrick approaches Henry and
gives him a slap on the back.

                    PATRICK
          Nice, dude.

                    HENRY
          She is such a cun--

Stephanie walks right in front of Henry, disgusted by his
language.

                    HENRY (CONT'D)
          Cunning...cunning, creature.

Stephanie shakes her head and hurries away.

Henry wrings his face in his hands.

Bruno observes the whole event in the near distance and
saunters in his office with a grin.

                    PATRICK
          For sure you ain't poking Holypoke now.

                    HENRY
          I never say "Cunt", except around you.

Another girl walks by in disgust at Henry.

                    HENRY
          You did it again.

The Bell RINGS again.

INT. DUSTER - AFTERNOON

CLOSE UP: An old WRISTWATCH.

Riva looks at his watch. Riva and Needa are dressed in
GOODWILL CLOTHES. They are so hip, they are ahead of their
time.

Needa rocks out to the RADIO. Riva is annoyed.

                    RIVA
               (in Arabic)
          How much further is this fucking Spokane
          place!

                    NEEDA
          English! Only English, otherwise they
          will know we are the ones.

Riva glances at a piece of paper.

>   RIVA
>   This...Henry, must be very clever, posing
>   as student.

Needa tries to ignore him. Two hot young GIRLS pull
alongside their car on the desolate freeway. They keep pace,
smile and flirt. Riva notices.

>   RIVA
>   The whole country is the enemy. Their
>   smiles hide many bad things.

Needa can't resist the girls and grins his first smile.

>   RIVA (cont'd)
>   Do not look at them.

The passenger side girl whips up her top and flashes her
perfect breasts as the driver speeds away laughing.

Needa blushes.

>   NEEDA
>   I do not think they were hiding anything
>   bad.

>   RIVA
>   You see what happens when girl keeps
>   clitoris!

Needa shakes his head at Riva and smiles to himself.

INT. SCULPTURE CLASS

Henry diligently works on a BUST of himself.

Students mold and create at their respective workstations.
Henry is proud of his work and hopes Stephanie will notice.
She doesn't.

Bruno saunters in wearing his trademark leather sandals. He
turns on MUSIC for the students.

>   BRUNO
>   Let your mind expand!

Patrick FARTS.

>   BRUNO
>   Your mind Patrick.

Henry turns around and smiles. Melody hops over to assist
Henry on his impressive project. Stephanie proudly works on
an amazing nearly life sized EAGLE that looks professional.
Bruno saunters by Stephanie.

                    BRUNO (CONT'D)
          Looks like you've done this before.

                    STEPHANIE
          Couple of times.

                    BRUNO
          Support that span.

Bruno points to the Eagle's span. Stephanie nods.

Henry overhears students talking about upcoming trips,
hearing buzz words like "AMSTERDAM", "PARIS" and "ROME".

                    HENRY
          Dude, check it out.

Henry splays his hands at his bust to Patrick. Melody
continues to fine touch his bust.

                    HENRY (CONT'D)
          Yours looks like shit. What's that
          supposed to be?

                    PATRICK
          It's my Mustang.

                    HENRY
          After you wrecked it?

Patrick throws a small ball of clay at laughing Henry.

                    HENRY (CONT'D)
          Speaking of shit. I'll be right back.

Henry takes off his smock and exits. Melody goes back to her
work area.

Patrick has a devilish grin and quickly makes something and
puts it on the lips of the Henry bust.

Henry bounces back in the room. Some students snicker at
Henry's bust. He wonders what the commotion is until he sees
that Patrick has formed an 8 inch girthy clay PENIS and
rested it on the bust's lips.

Henry thinks it's kind of funny but quickly removes it and
hurls it back at Patrick who catches it and puts it where his
own penis is, and waggles it.

                         PATRICK
               Hey, be nice to it dude.

Many students laugh, except for Stephanie still diligently
working on her eagle.

The bell RINGS. Patrick takes his FRISBEE out of his
backpack.

                         PATRICK (CONT'D)
               Let's round a crew to play Ultimate in
               Cascini.

                         HENRY
               Sounds good.

Patrick flips a short toss to Henry. Henry zips it back and
puts away his things.

Patrick is ready to throw it back. Henry creeps closer to
Stephanie's project to admire her work.

                         PATRICK
               Fitzpatrick!

Patrick flips the frisbee hard. Henry is not ready. He
instinctually jumps out of the way. The FRISBEE sails toward
unsuspecting Stephanie holding her EAGLE and rips through the
body of the eagle, leaving Stephanie holding only one WING.

Henry is stunned at the catastrophe and drops his backpack to
help.

                         STEPHANIE
               Just stay away!

She turns her back on him. He is helpless and rushes back
to his project.

                         HENRY
               Stephanie...Steph, look!

Henry takes both of his fists and karate chops them into
either side of his life-like bust, finishing up with a sock
in his nose, ruining his own project. She is still pissed
and puts the remnants on the shelf and hurries out of the
room.

                         HENRY (CONT'D)
               Fuck dude.

                         PATRICK
               You should've caught it, pinner.

They stumble out of the classroom. Henry is dejected holding the frisbee. Melody chuckles at the whole scene.

INT. PENSIONE BELLETINI - HENRY'S ROOM - DAY

A POSTER of Kelly LeBrock in a bikini hangs on the ceiling. Henry and Patrick lie on their respective beds staring at the ceiling in their new personalized, poster-ridden room. Henry's journal lies on his chest.

> PATRICK
> I mean if they didn't have a box, why would you care?

> HENRY
> Because guys smell and fart and girls clean shit up.

Henry throws dirty UNDERWEAR from his bedpost at Patrick. It lands on his face. Patrick whips it off.

> PATRICK
> Some of those SBD's on the bus were not from dudes.

> HENRY
> I wish I could wine and dine her. At least I'd have a chance.

> PATRICK
> I thought *they* were just here to get laid?

Henry gets up to leave.

> HENRY
> (like his parents)
> I want this place clean when I get back.

> PATRICK
> I'll get right on that.

Patrick raises up his legs, puts a lighter to his butt and FARTS, creating a blue streak. Henry smirks, shakes his head and leaves.

EXT. FLORENCE STREET

Henry walks dejected around the city. He admires the incredible BUILDINGS and elaborate WINDOW DISPLAYS. He finds himself on the other side of the Arno near SAN MINEATO CHURCH.

A THUNDERSTORM crashes out of nowhere, deluging RAIN on T-shirt clad Henry.

A VESPA roars up from behind. It's Melody, sporting only a wind breaker as protection.

                    MELODY
          Get on!

Henry gladly hops on. They charge through the rain laughing at the elements, happy to be alive.

SERIES OF SHOTS IN THE RAIN:

WINDING ROAD- Their Vespa races by the Hotel Cora and Bello Sguardo.

PARKING LOT- Their Vespa spins around the exterior of Fort Belvedere.

TREE LINED AVENUE- The THUNDER booms, the RAIN pounds even harder. Melody pulls over to an ancient portico. They hop off to the shelter and start to shiver.

INT. ANCIENT PORTICO

                    HENRY
          That was a blast! Thanks.

Henry takes off his shirt and wrings it. She checks out his toned body. They both still shiver and instinctively hold each other. Their eyes lock. They kiss, passionately.

In the shadows, Henry takes off her wet clothes and slips out of his shorts.

They proceed to make love.

Time passes. A carabinieri pulls up and shines his flashlight on the two. Henry covers her. He BARKS something at them.

                    HENRY
          Ok, Ok.

They quickly put their damp clothes on, giggling about being busted.

EXT. FLORENCE STREET - SUNSET

The rain has stopped for now. Henry and Melody ride up in front of the school still damp. Henry gets off, French kisses her and waves goodbye.

                         HENRY
          Tomorrow. Sounds good.

She speeds off. Patrick approaches.

                         PATRICK
          If I didn't see it with my own eyes. You
          got the fat chick and moped all at once.
          Amazing.

Patrick pats Henry on the back. Henry can't speak. He can't
even smile.

                         HENRY
          Yeah.

Henry walks away from Patrick inside the Palazzo. Patrick
shrugs and walks down the street.

Stephanie, writing on the protected Church steps across the
street, witnesses the entire event.

INT. PADRE BRUNO'S OFFICE - DAY

Henry walks into Bruno's office sad and dejected. Bruno
stands painting an oil PAINTING of Florence. He turns around
and laughs at his appearance.

                         BRUNO
          Well, look what the cat dragged in.

Bruno wipes his hands and hands him a towel. Henry dries his
hair. Bruno resumes painting.

                         HENRY
          Why are you only allowed to like the
          girls you're supposed to like.

                         BRUNO
          Ooh. This is good.

Bruno puts his brush down.

Henry is frustrated.

                         HENRY
          I mean, and you, they tell you, you can't
          bang girls. What a bunch of shit. No one
          way is right.

                         BRUNO
          I agree.

Henry is shocked at his agreement but continues begging for
an argument to get some answers.

                    HENRY
          And, Mary had a cherry. Like she didn't
          get laid by Joseph in several barns. You
          think he was some nice guy who wanted to
          hang out with her for twenty years? He
          needed some action.

Henry makes a bucking motion with his hips. Bruno smiles, he
can't believe how bold and real Henry is being, and he loves
it.

                    BRUNO
          I'm sure he did.

                    HENRY
          I mean how can any ONE religion be right?
          Did someone come down on a spaceship and
          tell everyone this stuff? We made it up!
          The 10 commandments are just common
          sense.

                    BRUNO
          Sounds like that Bible with a bomb
          exploded something inside you.

                    HENRY
          I mean that Holocaust shit was fucked up
          and all! But if everyone just sat down
          and had a beer with each other, none of
          that shit would've happened. I mean why
          are they still trying to get them?

                    BRUNO
          That's a whole different story. After the
          war, the Brits and the Allies gave away
          Palestinian land to the Jews as kind of
          an apology for all the atrocities that
          they did very little to stop.

                    HENRY
          How could they do that?

                    BRUNO
          They just did it. Palestine was a British
          colony. Back when everyone was (a al
          Robin Leach) "snatching up countries
          calling them their own". They gave back
          Hong Kong, Panama, but not this one.

                    HENRY
          Whoa! I'd be pissed too.

                    BRUNO
They tried to divide it equally after the
war, but the Palestinians who had been
there for the last 1700 years said "no
way", and because of that ended up with
nothing.

                    HENRY
What a bitch slap to them.

                    BRUNO
The Brits tried keeping the peace for a
while, but they were getting killed too
so they jumped ship. The war was over for
them. The Jews weren't going to lay down
this time. They learned what that got
them.

                    HENRY
It's totally like "Delta Force" there
now.

                    BRUNO
Add to that a few minor exclusionary
things like you can't own land unless
you're Jewish and--

                    HENRY
That's tight. So they went from victims
to full on perpetrators.

                    BRUNO
Not completely different from your
country taking land from the Indians,
except those guys are still fighting
back.

                    HENRY
That was two hundred years ago.

                    BRUNO
Hey, everybody is on their own evolution.

                    HENRY
So on religion dude, how can YOU dedicate
YOUR life to something you can shoot so
many holes in?

                    BRUNO
Faith.

                    HENRY
Was that the name of some nun you poked?

Bruno chuckles.

> BRUNO
> The church took me in when my mother
> died.

Henry loses some of his agitation.

> HENRY
> What do you owe them?

> BRUNO
> I can help searching souls like you. I
> get meaning from that. That's how I'm
> leaving my mark on the world.

> HENRY
> Well I'm searching for a sweet girl with
> a rocket body who loves guys named Henry.
> So get to work.

> BRUNO
> Why does she have to have a rocket body?

> HENRY
> How do you know already? I'm ruined.

> BRUNO
> Relax. You can't rush love, life or death
> for that matter.

> HENRY
> So if whatever is gonna happen is gonna
> happen. Why do I give a shit?

> BRUNO
> Aaahh, but that's just it. You do give a
> shit, and you can't change that. That
> shines through no matter what you do, or
> who you do, in your case.

> HENRY
> Why doesn't everyone else follow the
> golden rule.

> BRUNO
> How boring if everyone did?

Henry feels he's got him now.

> HENRY
> So when someone murders someone, that has
> truth and meaning?!

                    BRUNO
        It reminds you that it is terribly wrong.
        People die for a reason and evolve the
        world somehow when they do. There's a
        new generation everyday that needs to be
        reminded of what's right and wrong.

                    HENRY
        Guess that applies to racism and a bunch
        of other shit. Feeling left out sucks.

                    BRUNO
        Sei molto intelligente!

Bruno hugs Henry, but quickly releases wiping his wet hands
on his jeans.

                    HENRY
        Does that mean I'm getting an "A" in art?

                    BRUNO
        We'll see how your work is.

Bruno goes back to painting his SCENE OF FLORENCE.

                                        CUT TO:

INT. DUSTER - DAY

Needa POV: A snowy VIEW OF SPOKANE through the windshield.

Needa looks at a MAP. They approach Spokane from Sunset Hill
and descend in to the mountain city. An uncreative BILLBOARD
reads: WELCOME TO SPOKANE, A GREAT PLACE.

                    RIVA
        What is so great?

                    NEEDA
        Leave freeway here.

Riva exits the freeway and continues down the road.

                    RIVA
        When we arrive, we must be quick. Find
        him. Kill him. If anyone stops us, we
        kill them.

                    NEEDA
        Abu says just Henry.

                    RIVA
        They are all the enemy. What is the
        address?

Needa holds the address but doesn't want to give it to him.

> NEEDA
> Maybe we find girl from car first, then
> we kill Henry later.

> RIVA
> Gib me da address!

> NEEDA
> All the time you are so serious.

Needa dangles the paper at Riva. Riva snatches it from his hand and glances at it while driving. Riva U-turns around the median and parks in front of Bart's college house.

Riva takes one more look at the PRINTOUT. It shows "Henry Fitzpatrick CIA", and a PICTURE of Henry's father.

> RIVA
> Guns...Henry...kill!

> NEEDA
> (sheepishly)
> OK.

Riva puts the car in park; grabs the keys; hops out and heads to the trunk. Needa is stuck in his jammed seat belt, pushing his body back and forth trying to make it release.

EXT. CARSIDE

Riva opens the trunk.

> SMASH TO:

A snow ball SMACKS Riva square in the temple. Riva is startled and on the defensive, jerking his face toward its origin. Tabitha, dressed in a sheepskin coat and jeans, laughingly ducks in front of Riva. Riva is snowballed square in the face again.

> RIVA
> (in Arabic)
> Damnit!

> TABITHA
> I am soooo sorry.

Tabitha gently flicks the snow out of Riva's hair and face. Riva jumps back and finishes wiping the snow with a scowl. Tabitha quits trying to console him and steps to Needa who continues to fumble with his seat belt.

Bart, dressed in his trademark tight blue-jeans, stomps
toward a now wide-eyed fearful Riva.

                    BART
          Hey pardner, Bart Winslow. Put'er there.

Bart takes Riva's forearm and forces him to shake hands with
him, nearly lifting him off the ground with his unchecked
super strength.

                    BART
          Sorry bout that. Tabitha was jumping all
          around like a crazy raccoon. Ya'all
          gotta come inside for a cold one and warm
          up.

                    RIVA
          No.

Only Riva sees the GUNS in the trunk.

                    BART
          Ain't nothing as important as a free
          frosty. Get your buddy and git on in
          here!

                    RIVA
          No.

Riva looks disgustedly to Needa still desperately wriggling,
caught in his seat belt. He panics.

                    RIVA
          Where is this Henry?! Henry Fitzpatrick.

                    BART
          Shit fire! You are buddies of Henry's
          from It-all-E. Now, I ain't taking "no"
          for an answer.

Bart crouches down and effortlessly throws Riva over his
shoulder like a sack of potatoes; closes the trunk with his
free hand and heads up the stairs of the Craftsman style
home.

Riva is awed by Bart's strength and looks helplessly back at
Needa in the car.

Tabitha opens Needa's car door. She sexily leans over Needa
with her fresh breasts and long hair; pushes the jammed LATCH
together and releases awestruck Needa.

                    TABITHA
          Poor thing, must not have these back in
          Italy. Come on now sweetie, come inside
          with me.

Tabitha takes speechless Needa by the hand and stands him up.
She scans his funky grunge-esque hipster clothes.

                    TABITHA
          I heard you Italians were snappy
          dressers.

Tabitha leads him inside like a helpless boy. Needa isn't
completely convinced and brushes his clothes wondering if she
is making fun of him.

INT. BART'S LIVING ROOM

Bart's house is filled with laughing students, foosball, a
ping-pong table and a bar made out of steel kegs.

Needa spies Riva with Bart over near the bar. Tabitha
seduces Needa to sit down on the couch.

                    RIVA
          What is this frosty you drink so much of?

                    BART
          Vitamin R!... It's good for ya.

Bart flexes his bicep. Riva admires.

                    RIVA
          Is it alcohol?

                    BART
          Ya want some alcohol? I'm sure I got
          some whiskey round heres somewhere.

                    RIVA
          Alcohol is against my religion.

                    BART
          Mine too. Makes me crazy!

Riva looks quizzically at two drunk guys doing a beer BONG.

                    RIVA
          What is this?

                    BART
          Wanna try it?

Bart stomps over to the two guys, borrows the BONG and returns to Riva.

                    BART
          Lemme show ya how it's done.

Bart deftly takes a beer and empties it into the funnel while plugging the hole with his free thumb.

                    BART
          It's one...two...three.

Bart expertly finishes the beer bong in seconds and lets out a loud BURP.

                    BART
          Now it's your turn.

Bart prepares the beer bong and holds it for Riva.

                    RIVA
          Will it make me strong like you?

Riva rams the hose to his mouth as Bart lets his thumb go. Beer gushes out the sides of Riva's mouth.

                    BART
          Gotta relax buddy, but that was a good
          first timer. Let's try it again.

Bart loads up another beer into the bong. Needa smiles at Riva. Riva shrugs.

                    GUY #1
          Hey who's up next?

A guy holds a ping pong paddle. Bart holds his finger high pointing down to Riva anxiously holding the beer bong.

Tabitha walks Needa upstairs.

INT. STAIRWELL

                    TABITHA
          So you're family is from Syria
          originally, but now Palestine, Israel.
          Is that near Rome?

                    NEEDA
          My family is all dead now.

                    TABITHA
          Oh baby, I'm so sorry.

Tabitha standing one step higher on the stairs, kisses him.

                    TABITHA
          Let me show you something.

INT. BEDROOM - SPOKANE

Time passes.

Tabitha and Needa sit on the bed sharing a PHOTO ALBUM.

                    TABITHA
          And that's Henry and I double water-
          skiing.

Tabitha looks at Needa's face.

                    TABITHA
          It's like you've never seen him before.

                    NEEDA
          No it's that. He looks so young.

Tabitha turns the page, a PHOTO falls out.

                    TABITHA
          I love this one with his Mom and Dad.

Needa grabs the picture. He SUPERIMPOSES himself and his own
family in the PHOTO and rubs his eyes. Henry is finally
human to him.

                    TABITHA
          His dad just died too. He was the
          coolest, not around too much, but...

Needa can't speak. He looks at Tabitha. She kisses him
again.

INT. HENRY'S ROOM

Henry looks at the same framed PHOTO as Tabitha on his
bedstand. The sound of a SQUEAKING BED and MOANING fills the
room through the wall. Patrick throws a baseball up in the
air while lying on his back.

                    HENRY
          Dude this is burnt. Everybody is outta
          here every weekend and the little poor
          boys are left to duke it out with 200
          Italian guys for the 5 girls that put
          out.

                    PATRICK
        Where's Chunky this weekend.

                    HENRY
        Fuck you. Rome. She's the coolest one
        here.

Patrick backs off.

                    HENRY
        I can't stand it anymore. Let's get out
        of here.

INT. BART'S LIVING ROOM - NIGHT

Bart's house is in a full swing jam-packed party. Suggest
"Living in America" (James Brown) BLASTING out of large black
speaker. Riva and Needa are rip-roaring drunk, laughing and
dancing with other smiling Americans, arm in arm, kicking
their legs in the air.

                    NEEDA
                (singing loudly)
        Libbing in America!

                    RIVA
                (singing)
        Eye to eye...station to station.

                    NEEDA
                (yelling)
        America is the best!

                    RIVA
        Is not too bad.

A party girl dressed in stars and stripes leggings shimmies
behind Riva who ineptly follows her groove. They have never
had so much fun in their lives.

INT. BART'S LIVING ROOM - MORNING

Beer cans, pretzels and trash litter the shag carpeted floor.
Riva sleeps in a chair next to the stars and stripes girl who
is passed out face down on the floor like a Jim Jonestown
victim.

Needa and Tabitha sleep naked under a blanket on the couch.
Bart CLANGS in the kitchen. Needa wakes up and slips away
from comatose Tabitha, putting on his pants and then waking
up Riva.

                         NEEDA
                    (whispering)
               Wake up. We must talk.

Riva wakes up startled

                         RIVA
               Wha..wha..

Riva rubs his sore head.

                         NEEDA
               Come with me.

Riva follows behind Needa. Needa leans down and kisses
Tabitha on the cheek before leaving. Riva looks down
jealous.

                         RIVA
               We are not here to sleep with the enemy.

Needa puts his finger over Riva's lips. Riva bats it away.

EXT. BART'S PORCH

                         NEEDA
               You know. Henry does not live here. He
               is in Italy.

                         RIVA
               Why did Abu send us here?

Riva struggles to stay warm and jumps up and down.

                         NEEDA
               Think for yourself. Abu is not always
               right, dude.

Riva gets angrier.

                         RIVA
               Dude, what is dude?

                         NEEDA
               It is word you can put at beginning and
               end of sentence. I hear them.

                         TABITHA (O.S.)
               I need Needa!

Needa opens the door.

                         NEEDA
               Back in 15 minutes baby.

EXT. STREET

Riva and Needa walk to the corner telephone booth rubbing
their hands together to keep warm.

                    RIVA
          We must leeb now.

                    NEEDA
          What about our new friends? And Tabitha?

                    RIVA
          If dey knew truth, they would not be our
          friends.

                    NEEDA
          I am not leebing!

                    RIVA
          You are leebing with me when I say.

                    NEEDA
          You can go. Go work for Abu! I quit!

                    RIVA
          You can no quit! We train very hard. Abu
          will kill you.

                    NEEDA
          You maybe train very hard. I...I no pay
          much attention. I am no good as fighter.
          I am a lover!

                    RIVA
          I like it very much here too, drinking
          the Vitamin R and playing with the young
          girls breasts. But they help our enemy
          to take our country away. You know this!

                    NEEDA
          These people here did not disgrace our
          country. They do not even know our
          country. They barely know what goes on
          in their own country.

                    RIVA
          Then they will learn about our people and
          our cause or they can all die!

Riva makes a fist. Needa grabs his fist and lowers it.

                    NEEDA
          The Koran says you must know it is wrong
          beforehand to have committed real evil.

Riva thinks about it.

                    RIVA
          You just made that up.

Riva relaxes a bit but is still exasperated.

Needa shrugs.

                    NEEDA
          But is pretty good, huh?

                    RIVA
          How can we make them know our cause?

                    NEEDA
          Our cause! Yes! I will NEVER understand
          how the Jews take our sacred land. But I
          am also told when they arrive, most of
          the land they took you wouldn't want your
          best goat to graze on. And America, they
          help support Israel to fight against us!
          The only people who know about this is
          the government. The people, they will
          never want to know about it. They want
          to know about...

Needa does a football block against motionless Riva who
listens intently.

                    NEEDA (cont'd)
          This football, and good price on the Rain
          Dogs. Not these things we know.

                    RIVA
          But they make our people without homes.

                    NEEDA
          We are not only place in world with
          problems. I reed the TIME magazine on
          couch with Tabitha.

                    RIVA
          They kill your parents and mine!

                    NEEDA
          Your aunt tell me your mother choked on
          an olive pit.

                    RIVA
               (sheepishly)
          It was a Jewish restaurant.

Needa becomes more earnest.

                    NEEDA
          In America, I see many people from all
          over world come to live, people no get
          angry and kill them.

                    RIVA
          Yes, but they make people like us scrub
          their floors and wash their dishes.

                    NEEDA
          Until they hab dare own floor and dishes.

                    RIVA
          You are becoming one of them!

                    NEEDA
          And you are too. You can no kill
          innocent people anymore. Killing their
          camel will not give you a camel.

                    RIVA
          You are getting very bad with your
          examples.

                    NEEDA
          We must call Abu to tell him the truth.

Needa puts his arm around Riva and heads toward the phone
booth. Riva is initially startled by his arm, but then
welcomes their new relaxed camaraderie.

                    RIVA
          You are my best friend, you know that.

Needa nods.

INT. PHONE BOOTH

Riva and Needa smash in to the small phone booth, fumbling
about for the phone number. Needa dials while Riva jumps up
and down rubbing his hands together freezing.

                    NEEDA
          You are jumping around like the night I
          take your sister. Stop it.

Riva socks Needa. Needa smirks.

                    RIVA
          You are liar. You only kiss.

INT. ABU'S OFFICE -SUNSET

                    AL-BANRI
          His master Abu's office. How can I help
          you?

Needa rolls his eyes and covers the phone.

                    NEEDA
                 (whispering)
          It's hole licker Al-Banri.

Needa uncovers the phone.

INTERCUT AS NEEDED

                    NEEDA (cont'd)
          May I speak to Abu, this is Needa, it is
          very important.

                    AL-BANRI
          If you have something to say to him, you
          can tell me first.

                    NEEDA
          The Henry Fitzpatrick is no here. He is
          in Italy. He is not CIA, you make big
          mistake.

                    AL-BANRI
          But I get address of his home.

Al-Banri puts his thumb to his chest.

                    NEEDA
          Of his friend's home. You really fucked
          the goat on this one.

Abu walks in picking his teeth, rubbing his belly. He burps.

Abu mouths "who is it?". Al-Banri is nervous for his own
fate.

                    AL-BANRI
          Thank you very much for that information.
          We will take it from here.

Al-Banri hangs up the phone. He tries to play it cool.

                    AL-BANRI
          That was Needa and Riva.

                    ABU
          Mission completed?

                         AL-BANRI
          No, he escaped to Italy.

                         ABU
          Really. We will send our best allies for
          him.

                         AL-BANRI
          It must be me!

                         ABU
          If anyone gets the frequent flier miles
          it will be me.

Al-Banri pouts. Abu picks up the phone. Al-Banri prays he
doesn't discover the truth.

INT. HALLWAY - PENSION BELLETINI

A twenty something ARAB MAN enters carrying a brown canvas
GYM BAG. He scans the lobby and places the bag in a corner
near the leather couch. The BAG TAG reads HENRY FITZPATRICK.
The man quickly leaves.

EXT. PIAZZA SIGNORIA - FLORENCE

Henry and Patrick people-watch while eating their GELATO with
tiny white spoons. Patrick's frisbee is under his arm.

                         HENRY
          Thanks for the gelato dude.

                         PATRICK
          My pleasure man. At least I'm glad
          you're here.

                         HENRY
          Me too.

Henry and Patrick toast their cups.

INT. LOBBY -PENSIONE BELLETINI

A GYPSY enters the lobby with a bulging knapsack. He spies
the unattended bag and beelines for it. Just then, SILVANO
(45), the burly good-looking owner of the pensione, sees the
gypsy. The gypsy grabs the bag and runs like hell. Silvano
runs after him out the door yelling.

                         SILVANO
                    (in Italian)
          You piece of shit! You better run!

Silvano is steaming and calls the police.

EXT. PENSION BELLETINI

Henry and Patrick toss the frisbee while walking down the
street. The gypsy hauls ass down the street right in between
their play.

                    PATRICK
          Wow dude! He's fast.

They stop playing and run up the stairs of the pensione.

INT. LOBBY -PENSIONE BELLETINI

Silvano stands waiting for an answer on the other line.

                    SILVANO
          Damn Carabinieri!

                    HENRY
          Che fai Silvano.

                    SILVANO
               (heavy accent English)
          Damn gypsy stole something from the lobby
          here.

A loud ground shaking BOOM! rattles the ground like an
earthquake.

                    HENRY
          Holy shit! What was that?

Tom and Kate come out of their room looking freshly sexed. A
STUDENT runs in the lobby from outside.

                    STUDENT #1
          You guys, come check it out! This guy
          blew himself up in the piazza.

The student turns around and runs back toward the mayhem.
Tom makes an "oooh" face at Henry as they all head out the
door.

INT. ABU'S OFFICE

Abu stands furiously talking on the telephone while Al-Banri
sits attentively nearby.

                    ABU
          What do you mean the bomb blew up a
          gypsy! I will come kill him myself!

Abu slams the phone down. Al-Banri jumps up.

                              AL-BANRI
                    I can identify him.

Abu thinks for a moment.

                              ABU
                    OK. But no room service this time, no
                    movies, no nothing. We are freedom
                    fighters not playboys.

Al-Banri nods.

EXT. BART'S HOUSE - AFTERNOON

Riva and Needa slowly walk up the stairs of Bart's house and
enter.

INT. BART'S HOUSE

Needa sits on the couch with Tabitha. Riva stands nearby.

                              NEEDA
                    We must talk to Henry.

                              TABITHA
                    Don't look so worried baby.

Tabitha walks in the kitchen, they follow.

INT. KITCHEN

                              TABITHA
                    I know Bart has their number right here.

Tabitha points to a large yellow stickie on the wall. She
dials the phone. The kitchen is a shambles from the party
and Bart's breakfast creation.

INT. PENSIONE BELLETINI - NIGHT

Adriane walks over to pick up the ringing wall phone. She is
in her bathrobe with a facial clay mask and her hair in a
towel.

                              ADRIANE
                    Pronto?

INTERCUT AS NEEDED

A bag of "Prontos" chips lies near Tabitha. She is amazed at
Adriane's telepathy and crunches in to a chip.

                              TABITHA
                    Adriane?!(squeal) It's Tabitha!

                    ADRIANE
Oh my God! Tabby cat, how are you?

                    TABITHA
Doing guh-rate! Met a couple of your
Italian throwbacks.

                    ADRIANE
Really?! I haven't had any to throw back,
yet.

                    TABITHA
You still doing that semi-virgin thing?

                    ADRIANE
Did Henry tell you that?

                    TABITHA
Where is that dirty dog?

                    ADRIANE
There was some big "boom" and they all
ran out of here.

                    TABITHA
So tell him to give us a call here at
Bart's.

                    ADRIANE
You got it. I'll have him call you. Ciao.

                    TABITHA
We're fixing to do that right now. Buh-
bye.

Tabitha goes to the fridge and opens up both doors.

                    TABITHA
We're going to have to fatten you boys
up.

INT. BRUNO'S OFFICE - EVENING

Henry, Patrick and Tom stand excitedly talking over Bruno's
shoulder while he carefully works.

                    PATRICK
--Should of seen it Bruno. There was
"body" everywhere.

                    BRUNO
You guys need to be more careful.

Bruno places another dot of liquid on a EURAIL PASS with a dropper.

                    BRUNO
          Step two.

Another dot.

                    BRUNO (cont'd)
          Three...Viola!

Bruno wipes the Eurail clean with a tissue and hands it to Henry.

                    BRUNO
          Who's next.

                    HENRY
          Where'd you get this stuff?

Henry marvels at Bruno's precision on his EURAIL.

                    BRUNO
          France, they use it to remove ink from
          clothes, but as you can see it has other
          uses.

Tom shoves his Eurail under Bruno' nose.

                    BRUNO (CONT'D)
          This ought to keep you up with some of
          the rich kids.

Bruno meticulously works on Tom's Eurail Pass.

                    HENRY
          You're the best Bruno.

                    BRUNO
          And if you get busted, you're all on your
          own.

Henry hugs Bruno.

                    BRUNO
          I noticed you three haven't signed up for
          my fund-raiser for the orphanage.

                    TOM
          Dude, we're not selling cookies.

                    BRUNO
          All you have to do is get drunk.

Patrick high fives Tom and Patrick.

                    PATRICK
          We can do that.

EXT. PENSION BELLETINI -AFTERNOON

Henry and Melody walk arm and arm with Tom, Patrick and Kate
out the front door of the pensione carrying small bags.

A blue shiny PORSCHE pulls up. The window rolls down.
Adriane pokes her head out.

                    ADRIANE
          Here's the address of the pad at the
          beach. Give me a call when your train
          gets in.

Henry snatches the paper. The Porsche SQUEALS away almost
hitting Al-Banri who is busy looking at a MAP of Florence.
He jumps out of the way and then notices Henry. His eyes
widen and then sharpen.

Henry and gang saunter past Al-Banri, not even noticing him.

Al-Banri turns to follow them as they continue to the train
station. He places his hand on his knapsack outlining a GUN.

INT. SANTA MARIA NOVELLA TRAIN STATION - FLORENCE

Henry and his gang walk down the platform towards the 2nd
class car. He notices Nella, Stephanie and Nancy struggling
with their Louis Vuitton luggage climbing in to a 1st class
car. Stephanie jumps on first, then Nella who ignores Nancy.
Nancy struggles with her luggage. Al-Banri waits back 200
feet.

                    NANCY
          Nella, can you help?

                    NELLA
          I told you not to bring so much.

The train WHISTLE blows. The loudspeaker announces their
departure. Nancy panics. Henry steps in.

                    HENRY
          Hey Nance, why not come sit with us?

                    NANCY
          Oh hurry Henry!

                    HENRY
          Relax.

Henry effortlessly grabs her stuff, hands Patrick a bag and
they all jump on the slow moving train, their car is 2nd
class. Al-Banri jumps on Nella's first class train.

INT. TRAIN COMPARTMENT

Henry puts away Nancy's things and makes a seat for her in
their cozy cabin. Nancy sits down next to gruff Kate and
smiles. Kate just stares at her.

                    NANCY
          You know that Nella, she's just not a
          very nice person sometimes.

                    HENRY
          Why not hang with us this weekend.

                    NANCY
          I just think I'll do that. A girl's got
          to try some new things sometime.

                    TOM
          Right on Nance.

Tom leans over and high-fives her.

Henry shakes his head at Patrick who holds two fingers
straight up trying unsuccessfully to wedge an opposing finger
in between them, because they're too tight.

INT. NELLA'S TRAIN CAR

Nella busily splays her things about her rail car, making it
like her home. Al-Banri appears at the door and begins to
sit down, moving some of Nella's things to one side.

                    NELLA
          Excuse me, this car is taken.

                    AL-BANRI
          You do not own the train.

Al-Banri sits down anyway. Nella is frustrated.

                    NELLA
               (to Stephanie)
          I can't believe Nancy is hanging out with
          them. She better watch it.

                    STEPHANIE
          Or what.

Stephanie looks at her stone faced. She begins to read her
book.

Nella starts looking at her compact mirror and primping. Al-Banri mocks her every move.

> NELLA
> (to Al-Banri)
> Can I help you?

> AL-BANRI
> Is free country, no?

Nella fumes. Al-Banri mocks her fuming.

TIME PASSES

Nella, Stephanie and Al-Banri nap. Nella has created a partition out of her school book so Al-Banri can't watch her face anymore. The train stops. They continue to doze.

EXT. TRAIN STATION

Henry and the gang hobble by their window. The train starts taking off. Nancy calls out.

> NANCY
> Bye Stephanie! I'll see you Monday.

Stephanie jumps up and struggles with the window, finally opening it. She sticks her head out, obviously sad, and a bit jealous of Nancy's impending fun.

> STEPHANIE
> Where are you going?

> NANCY
> With them!

She waves at the gang, including Henry. Henry waves back.

Nella sticks her head out.

> NELLA
> What about your soothing facial and mud
> pack?

> NANCY
> Take mine.

Al-Banri jumps up in a panic and realizes he's missed Henry. He runs to the train car window and looks out at his failure. The train picks up speed.

He returns to Nella's train car and sits down, crosses his arms and gives Nella an annoying smile.

EXT. BEACH - ANSEDONIA - DAY

Henry, Tom, Kate and Nancy traipse their bags and bedrolls
along the beautiful nearly deserted Mediterranean beach.

                    HENRY
          Well gang, this looks as good a place as
          any.

                    NANCY
          Oh my god, how embarrassing to show up at
          that man's place and get turned away!

                    PATRICK
          This will be good for you.

                    NANCY
          I've never slept outside! And there are
          animals!

                    HENRY
          Probably just a few rats and things.

                    NANCY
          I should have gone to the spa. I...I just
          can't handle this. We're going to get
          held up by bandits and raped, I just know
          it.

                    TOM
          Ya gotta lose it sometime.

TIME PASSES

The group huddles around a small campfire. The sun drops in
the Western sky. Nancy wears a LANZ OF SALZBURG nightgown.
Tom hands Nancy a COKE CAN fashioned in to a pipe and loads a
chunk of GREEN BUD. Henry cuddles and makes out with Melody.

                    NANCY
          You sure this isn't going to cause brain
          damage or anything.

                    TOM
          You'll be fine Nance, look at me!

Tom smiles with Chinese eyes as Nancy awkwardly takes a hit
and COUGHS.

INT. STEFANO'S LIVING ROOM - EVENING

Adriane coughs after doing a shot.

                    STEFANO
          You need another drink, and then we play
          a game. (to Paolo in Italian)Peek-a-boo
          with my sausage.

Stefano and Paolo laugh. Adriane is wasted and stares off
into space.

                    ADRIANE
          I really can't...(hiccup) I shouldn't
          have had the last three.

Stefano reaches down and callously grabs her breast. Adriane
is horrified and bats his hand away.

                    STEFANO
               (snickering)
          Those very nice.

Adriane looks around to Paolo for help but sees that he isn't
any.

                    STEFANO (CONT'D)
          We will have much more fun if you relax.

Paolo shrugs.

                    ADRIANE
          Paolo! Help me!

                    PAOLO
          He is my friend Adriane. We stay at his
          house.

Adriane is thunderstruck at being betrayed by her love.
Stefano reaches back into Adriane's blouse for another grab
and rips her blouse as his hand is batted away.

                    ADRIANE
          Get off of me!

Adriane jumps up in anger and pulls her shirt back together.

                    ADRIANE (CONT'D)
          Paolo! How could you?

                    PAOLO
          Very easily I thought. Look at the way
          you are dressed.

                    ADRIANE
          The way I'm dressed!

                    PAOLO
          You dress like a whore. I figure no
          problem.

Adriane looks down at her torn outfit, her mascara running.

                    ADRIANE
          I'm a..a..virgin. I...I loved you.

Adriane weeps stronger.

                    PAOLO
          Hymen, no hymen, what is difference. You
          American girls know you love the Italian
          cock.

Paolo grabs his crotch and smiles sinisterly.

Adriane spins around and rushes out of the room.

                    PAOLO (CONT'D)
               (In Italian)
          What did I say?

                    STEFANO
          You told me this American girl was easy.
          Why did you come down to my house.

                    PAOLO
          Maybe she is just playing hard to get.

Adriane storms out the front door wheeling her large suitcase
by a leash.

EXT. VILLA - FRONT PATIO

                    STEFANO
               (in English)
          You don't know what you're missing,
          stupid American girl.

Adriane continues walking briskly, wobbling momentarily from
the cobblestones on her high heels. She spins around.

                    ADRIANE
          Yeah! I think I can wait a lifetime for
          this!

Adriane holds up her pinky.

Paolo laughs.

Stefano hits Paolo.

                    STEFANO
                 (in Italian)
            What did you tell her.

                    PAOLO
            Nothing.

Paolo smirks, Stefano hits Paolo again in the arm.

EXT. ANSEDONIA BEACH

Tom looks over in the distance and spies Adriane storming
towards the beach with her wheeled suitcase in tow. Her
suitcase falls over. She drags it on the sand.

                    TOM
            Look! She got tossed too.

Adriane gets closer. Her suitcase won't wheel on the sand
and she leaves it to continue tromping toward the group in
her high heels.   It's obvious she has been crying, and her
shirt is ripped. Henry jumps to her aid.

                    HENRY
            Did that asshole do this to you? Tom,
            let's go.

                    ADRIANE
            No, no just forget it. How could I have
            been so stupid?

Adriane sits down and weeps. She pops her blue contacts out,
flicks them on the sand and puts on her glasses.

                    ADRIANE
            I really thought he liked me. How could
            I just let him put you guys out on the
            beach? You must hate me.

                    KATE
            Just a little.

Kate smiles at Adriane and hands her the Coke can for a hit
of marijuana.

NIGHT TIME:

All are nestled in their sleeping bags.

76.

                    ADRIANE
                (singing drunkenly)
        "Oh I wish I was an Oscar Mayer
        wiener...that is what I really wanna
        be... cause if I were an Oscar Mayer
        wiener...everyone would be EATING me.

                    KATE
        That's it.

Kate zips the bag over her head and snuggles back with Tom.

Adriane continues to sing zipped under the bag.

                    ADRIANE
                (muffled a la Pina Coloda
                 song)
        "If you like penis a-lot uh...and getting
        fucked in a truck.

Nancy giggles and gets into being stoned in her sleeping bag.

INT. SPA HOTEL ROOM - EVENING

Al-Banri sprawls on his bed picking his teeth after just
eating a huge dinner. He sighs and clicks on the remote for
the television.

INT. HENRY'S ROOM - FLORENCE - DAY

Their backpacks litter the room. Kate lies on her stomach
filing her nails with her feet in the air as Tom dumps a cup
full of SAND out of his shoe letting it run through his
fingers. Henry eagerly reads a pamphlet.

                    KATE
        The maids are gonna kick your ass.

                    TOM
        I miss it babe.

Tom pours some of the sand in his hair and shakes his head.

A KNOCK on the door. Patrick pokes his head in.

                    PATRICK
        Bruno wants us to help set up.

                    HENRY
        I'll let you two have a conjugal.

Henry grabs his coat and exits.

EXT. PENSIONE BELLETINI-FLORENCE

Henry and Patrick bounce out of the arched doorway. In the
outdoor cafe across the street sits Al-Banri, now dressed
elegantly, with shopping bags that read Gucci and Ferragamo
sitting by his side. Al-Banri quickly finishes his coffee
and jumps up following them encumbered by his many bags.
They arrive at the bar L'ANGELO AZZURO. Al-Banri realizes
he's useless and doesn't follow.

INT. L'ANGELO AZZURO BAR - FLORENCE - EVENING

CLOSE UP of a beer stein being filled with Heineken.

The Gonzaginis crowd the blue neon modern bar. Tables sit in
rows covered in beer pitchers. Bruno stands on a chair with
a STOPWATCH.

                    BRUNO
          OK, senti ragazzi! The object of 100
          shots night is to drink a shot every 60
          seconds. If you make it to 100, it's
          free! If you don't, we keep your $50
          bucks.

Bruno motions Nella over and puts his arm around her.

                    BRUNO
          Nella is donating an extra $20 for every
          person who completes it.

Nella crosses her arms and rolls up on the balls of her feet.

Students eagerly fill their shot glasses with Heineken and
prepare for their drunken journey. Bruno clicks the
stopwatch.

                    BRUNO (cont'd)
          Bottoms up! Come on Henry, this should
          be nothing for you.

Students slam their shots and quickly refill their glasses.

Al-Banri looks through the window, waiting outside with his
backpack.

TIME PASSES

Several students are passed out in their seats as sober Bruno
laughs, looking at his watch. It appears the orphans have
won.

                    BRUNO
          Number, Seventy Five.

Bruno motions with his thumb to guzzle. Everyone is stinking drunk, laughing, kissing, groping. The middle-aged bar OWNER is exasperated. He has never seen a group act like this.

The bathroom is backed up with people. Nancy is bombed, but tries to remain her composure in her monogrammed sweater. Melody refills everyone's mugs.

                    TOM
              (to Henry)
         Dude, I'm gonna blow.

Tom pulls Henry out to the curb. Al-Banri moves to the shadows and fiddles in his bag.

EXT. L'ANGELO AZZURO BAR

                    HENRY
         Here?

                    TOM
         Ready?

Al-Banri pulls his GUN out of his backpack and begins to take aim at Henry.

                    AL-BANRI
              (to himself)
         Ready.

An older smiling ITALIAN COUPLE, interested in the commotion, brushes in to Al-Banri, catching him off guard, scaring him. The couple becomes concerned when they come upon Henry and Tom hunched over.

                    TOM
         One...

                    HENRY
         Two.

                    TOM
         Three!

Beer rips out of Tom's innards. Henry is grossed out and laughing, easily following suit. They LAUGH hysterically, trying to one-up each other on distance. Stephanie looks out the window and sours her face, turning around. The Italian couple is horrified at the paradox and hurries away.

                    TOM
         Karen Carpenter was on to something. I
         out-shot you dude.

Tom points just as the bar owner comes out to angrily shoo them away.

> HENRY
> Let's get out of here.

> TOM
> Damn Orphans got my money!

Tom and Henry stumble down the ancient street, arm in arm. Al-Banri is furious. He puts his gun away, and follows.

EXT. PENSIONE BELLETINI

> TOM
> Fucking door's locked.

Tom bangs the door.

> TOM
> Fuck this!

Tom rocks the door and rips it open with a strong pull.

Tom and Henry gallop up the stairs. Al-Banri is pushed aside by the mob of drunk students from 100 shots nights.

INT. PENSIONE BELLETINI

Mayhem ensues. Someone brings out their boom box and puts on some OLD SCHOOL FUNK. (suggest Rick James "You and I") Everyone starts boogieing. Students raid the honor bar near the front desk and don't sign for anything. Silvano runs out from the back room in horror. Hot Adriane quickly grabs Silvano and dirty dances with him.

Nancy stumbles in, sweater in hand, her oxford shirt untucked. She dangles a small wooden handled purse. She carelessly tosses it on the couch and starts to happily jiggle offbeat to the music.

> SILVANO
> Che fai!

A girl taps Henry on the shoulder and points to the wall phone.

> HENRY
> (yelling)
> Who is it?

> GIRL
> Your friends in Spokane.

Henry jumps over to the phone and plugs his ear with one finger.

                    HENRY
          Is it Bart?

INT. BART'S HOUSE

                    TABITHA
          No! It's Needa, here!

Tabitha hands Needa the phone and goes into the kitchen.

INTERCUT AS NEEDED

                    HENRY
          What, you need a beer?

                    NEEDA
          Hello Henry, I must tell you, you are in
          great danger.

                    HENRY
          What Bart? I think that would be great
          if you wanted to bang her! That's cool
          dude, that was last year. She's her own
          woman.

                    NEEDA
          You must leave Florence now. They will
          try to kill you.

A cute girl grabs Henry to go dance.

                    HENRY
          It's too loud dude. I miss you too.
          Give Tabitha a good spanking for me. She
          loves that. Ciao for now.

Henry hangs up and goes back to boogie.

Tabitha walks back into the room.

                    NEEDA
          What is good spanking?

                    TABITHA
          This!

Tabitha gives Needa a firm swat on his butt. He jumps in surprise.

> TABITHA
> Did you get to tell him your important
> news?

> NEEDA
> I do not believe he understood. We must
> telephone again when is more quiet.

Tabitha caresses his face, hugs him and kisses him on the
lips.

> TABITHA
> Quiet. I like the sound of that.

Needa looks at Riva very concerned while hugging Tabitha.

INT. PENSIONE BELLETINI - FLORENCE

> HENRY
> Dude, where's Melody.

> TOM
> It's all you can eat at Pizza Pino.

Henry is not amused.

> TOM
> Kidding.

Henry runs downstairs.

EXT. PENSIONE BELLETINI-FLORENCE

Henry spies Melody walking arm in arm with an Italian man.
The man gives Melody a sloppy kiss. Henry jumps in front of
her.

> MELODY
> What are you doing?

She turns back to the man. Henry can't believe it. The man
continues to caress her.

> HENRY
> I can't believe it.

> MELODY
> Why don't you get on your moped with
> Patrick and find another fat chick.
> She'll appreciate it, right?

Henry in stunned.

Melody turns away. The Italian man is puzzled.

                         MELODY
              Non c'e' una problema. E' mio fratello.

Patrick stands at the doorway witnessing the event.

                         PATRICK
              Oooh, Dude, sorry.

INT. HOTEL ROOM - FLORENCE - EVENING

Al-Banri winces and holds the YELLING telephone away from his
head.

                         AL-BANRI
              This hotel is most close to Fitzpatrick.

The YELLING continues.

                         AL-BANRI
              I only buy the new clothes to look like
              the people.

The YELLING gets louder, Al-Banri winces.

                         AL-BANRI
              Do not worry, I will trace his every
              move.

The YELLING is short, and then a CLICK.

Al-Banri hangs up the phone, wets his index finger and shines
a spot on his new shoe. He clicks back on the TV with the
remote. He cuts in to his Bistecca Fiorentina and savors it
while watching an old episode of "All My Children".

                         AL-BANRI
              Erica, you are such a bitch. I love you.

EXT. PENSIONE BELLETINI - FLORENCE - MORNING

Sunglassed students groggily line up with their bags and
winter wear intent on a long weekend of skiing. Bruno checks
off their names as they enter the bus.

INT. WINDOW SILL

Al-Banri looks down from his hotel window with scorn. He
takes turn choosing different students in the SCOPE of his
gun.

POV: GUN SCOPE: Henry walks outside, hugging various
students.

Al-Banri quickly zips his bag and gathers his things.

EXT. PENSIONE BELLETINI

The students finish loading the bus. Bruno gets on, the
doors close and the bus takes off. Al-Banri follows in his
rented BMW.

INT. BUS - DAY

Students sit in their various cliques and nurse their hang-
overs and moan, relaxing to 80's MUSIC on the P.A. System.

Al-Banri's BMW is seen through the back window.

TIME PASSES

INT. AL-BANRI'S BMW

The bus encounters steep winding mountain roads. Al-Banri
looks up puzzled at the majestic peaks through the
windshield. A student sticks his head out of the bus and
PUKES on Al-Banri's windshield.

Al-Banri turns on the wipers which makes it worse.

The bus finally arrives in Cervinia, with a breathtaking view
of the Matterhorn in the background. Al-Banri parks nearby.

The students flood out of the bus, throwing snowballs, giddy
about the weekend.

Al-Banri stays in his car with his hands clenched on the
steering wheel, a bit scared of their enthusiasm.

INT. RED DRAGON LODGE -EVENING

The lobby teams with students. Al-Banri pushes his way to
the front desk.

                    FRONT DESK MAN
          Buona Sera, signore.

                    AL-BANRI
          One room please, deluxe with view.

                    FRONT DESK MAN
                (heavy accent)
          I am very sorry sir. We are fully
          booked.

The man senses the disappointment and tries to please.

                    FRONT DESK MAN (cont'd)
          But we do have one small room, near the
          elevator.

                    AL-BANRI
          I will take it.

Al-Banri presents his credit card. The man takes it and runs
it through the machine. It is denied.

                    FRONT DESK MAN
          I am very sorry sir. This card has been
          cancelled. We take travelers checks, and
          of course cash.

Al-Banri storms out to his BMW.

EXT. RED DRAGON LODGE

Al-Banri tries to start the engine. The battery is dead. He
bangs his hand on the wheel and attempts to get comfortable
for the evening, but is woefully unsuccessful.

EXT. RED DRAGON LODGE - MORNING

Al-Banri's BMW windows are frosted from the inside. Al-Banri
opens the door. He is blue from the cold.

Henry and several students mill near the rental center.
Henry, Tom and Patrick grab their skis and head toward the
long gondola lift line.

Al-Banri notices an unattended pair of skis and pink boots
unattended. He snags them.

EXT. NEAR GONDOLA

Al-Banri hurries near the long lift line, noticing how others
are putting on their boots. His boots are obviously women's
and are too small, but he makes them work.

Except for a small jacket, Al-Banri is completely unprepared
for skiing. He carries his small backpack while he
obnoxiously pushes through the line to be closer to Henry.
Nella and Stephanie crowd in with the line near Henry.

Al-Banri hides his face from Nella and Stephanie.

                    NELLA
               (to Patrick)
          I hope this mountain is big enough for us
          to not keep running into you dolts.

                    PATRICK
          It's just a little bit bigger than your
          ass Nella. Don't worry you wouldn't be
          able to keep up.

The Gondola doors slide open. The crowd surges forward. Al-Banri is one of the last to make it inside. The doors close.

INT. GONDOLA

The crowd makes OOOOOH and AAAAAAH sounds going over the rhytmic bumps created via the pylons. Al-Banri mocks the laughing and sounds of Henry and friends. Tom stares at Nella looking for a fight.

>   TOM
>   I don't get it. I mean usually fat girls
>   are really nice.

>   PATRICK
>   Or at least appreciative. There's
>   nothing worse than a fat bitch.

>   HENRY
>   You fuckers have gotten me in enough
>   trouble.

Henry backs away.

EXT. TOP OF THE MOUNTAIN

Al-Banri emulates them putting on their skis.

Henry, Tom and Patrick take off with a WOO-HOO!

Al-Banri pushes off and gains speed. He can't stop. He somersaults in a ball of skis and poles finally crashing in to a group ski lesson, sending them to the snow.

SERIES OF SHOTS: Suggest "Fire in the Twilight" Wang Chung

STEEP POWDER RUN- The Henry, Tom and Patrick carve expert figure eights down the mountain.

JUMP RUN- The three perform Daffies and Spread Eagles.

INT. ZERMATT SKI LODGE - DINING ROOM - ONE P.M.

Tom, Patrick, Henry, Kate and three girls analyze their menus and boisterously recap their day.

A commotion behind their table interrupts them. A large effeminate balding man (35) with a sunburned face and sweat on his brow, is enraged at the waiter. The waiter remains annoyingly calm.

                    35 YEAR OLD MAN
          I beg your pardon! I work very hard on
          my weigh---

                    WAITER
          Eska-to fatty-gay?

                    35 YEAR OLD MAN
          You French really have some nerve!

Henry jumps to the rescue with a smile.

                    HENRY
          Dude...relax. He's asking if you're
          tired, like fatigued.

The anger erases from the man's face and he smiles at the
waiter. The waiter smiles back. They are friends now.

                    35 YEAR OLD MAN
          Thank you so much young man.

                    HENRY
          No sweat.

Henry sits down, proud of his accomplishment. The waiter
approaches their table.

                    WAITER
               (heavy accent)
          Zee fat gay man wishes to buy all of your
          lunches.

Henry beams over to the man and gives a huge thumbs up.

                    HENRY
          Right on dude!

Henry smiles and shoots a hang loose sign back at the man.

                    TOM
          Gay men rule!

Kate looks quizzically at Tom.

TIME PASSES

Dirty plates and beer steins litter their table.

                    LOUDSPEAKER
          Tutti gli gente che allogiano a Cervinia
          devono partire addesso.

Students ignore the loudspeaker.

                    LOUDSPEAKER (CONT'D)
              (In French)
              (LOUDSPEAKER (CONT'D)
              (In German)
              (LOUDSPEAKER (CONT'D)
              (accented)
         All persons staying on the Cervinia side
         must leave immediately.

The waiter approaches. The loudspeaker systematically
repeats the message in the several languages.

                    WAITER
              I guess you must leave now.

                    HENRY
              What for?

                    WAITER
              Big storm coming. They do not want you
              stranded here.

                    PATRICK
              There's no storm.

Patrick motions his hand at the sunny window.

                    WAITER
              Down here, but the world is very
              different up there.

Patrick looks toward the peak and notices fast moving clouds
swirling, and a grey front approaching.

                    PATRICK
              Guess it's time to rumble.

The gang quickly gathers their things and heads for the tram,
thanking their lunch benefactor.

INT. LOWER TRAM BUILDING - ZERMATT

Henry and gang approach Nella, Stephanie, Nancy and her
entourage.

                    NELLA
              So, we even switched countries and we
              still run into you.

                    KATE
              I'm not listening to this crap on the way
              up.

                         NANCY
            Hi you guys! How was your day?

Nella looks at Nancy like she's on thin ice.

                    TRAM OPERATOR
            Everyone aboard!

Through the window, Al-Banri staggers in to the restaurant
frozen, bedraggled and beaten.

The group enters the tram. The doors shut and the tram
begins its ascent. Al-Banri scrambles up to the departing
tram in frustration.

INT. TRAM - ZERMATT

The tram continues up the sun drenched hill. Henry's and
Nella's gangs stand at opposite sides of the tram.

                         NELLA
            Such a gyp.

                    TRAM OPERATOR
            I hope we are not too late.

The operator looks ominously out the window up the hill. A
tram full of people descends past them.

The tram rocks wildly now engulfed in a white out.

                          TOM
            Whoa dude, gnarly. Remember when that
            tram fell at Squaw Valley.

Tom smashes one palm into the other. One of Nella's gang
begins to cry.

                         NELLA
            Shut up Asshole.

Even Tom is now terrified as the tram swings like windblown
clothes on a clothesline.

                    TRAM OPERATOR
            This is not good. We are too late. You
            must wait in the hut.

The tram BANGS into a pylon sending everyone off balance.
Everyone SCREAMS.

                         HENRY
            Can't we just reverse and go down!

The operator shakes his head. The students can barely make
out the hut that they are slowly approaching. The tram SLAMS
into the guiding rails, unable to enter its safety. The
students SHRIEK in horror. Henry helps steady terrified
Stephanie.

                    TRAM OPERATOR
          I must have silence!

The tram continues to bang wildly against either side of the
hut entrance. The operator expertly times the swinging and
guns the tram, finally entering the shelter.

                    TRAM OPERATOR (CONT'D)
          You must stay here until the storm
          passes.

                    HENRY
          Why don't you just take us down.

                    TRAM OPERATOR
          Instructions from management. They don't
          want to put you up for the night.

                    HENRY
          Those cheap bastards. How long do we
          have to wait up here?!

                    TRAM OPERATOR
          One hour, two hours, maybe all night. I
          am not God. These storms can kill.
          Blankets are in the closet.

                    RADIO (O.S.)
          Did you get rid of the Americans?

                    TRAM OPERATOR
          All disembarked. Ready for return.

                    NELLA
          You're not leaving us!

                    TRAM OPERATOR
          Be good to each other.

The tram door closes. It descends into the white.

                    NELLA
          I am not spending the night up here!
          Especially with you.

Nella glares at Henry and Patrick.

                    STEPHANIE
          Maybe it's not such a bad idea.

Patrick opens the dust laden closet and COUGHS. He returns
with an old skanky wool blanket resting it on Nella's head.
She bats it off her head in disgust.

                    NELLA
          If you want to spend the night with THEM,
          go right ahead.

                    PATRICK
          I didn't come here for this either.

                    TOM
          Come on. They're only rentals.

The students chuckle at the devilish logic and begin to
prepare their equipment. They SCRAPE their skis towards the
door.

Henry notes Stephanie's apprehensiveness as their eyes
connect.

                    PATRICK
          Last one down is a rotten egg. There's a
          warming hut with col' beer a half mile
          down.

Patrick swings the door open. The gale force wind and snow
rushes in. Patrick and Tom disappear into the white, quickly
followed by Nella and her entourage. Henry notices the
terror on Stephanie's face and SCRAPES his skis over to her.

                    HENRY
          You ready to try it? Don't worry, I'll
          make sure you get down.

Henry nods at Nancy.

                    HENRY (CONT'D)
          You too Nance.

Nancy fumbles with her equipment.

                    NANCY
          Thanks Henry.

The three SCRAPE their skis toward the white out.

EXT. MOUNTAIN TRAIL - CERVINIA

                    HENRY
               (yelling over the wind)
          OK! Stay low! This wind can lift you.

Henry trudges into the WHITE-OUT along the narrow 8 foot ski
ridge with sheer drop-offs on either side. He motions for the
other two to join. Stephanie and Nancy slowly fight against
the icy WIND.

Henry crouches to go down the hill and looks around one last
time to make sure all is well. Henry cranes his head around
Nancy to see Stephanie's SKIS pointed downward with Stephanie
missing. Nancy moves slowly toward Henry.

                    HENRY (CONT'D)
          Where's Stephanie?!

Nancy looks slowly behind herself and wigs out.

                    NANCY
          I don't know, but I'm freezing!

                    HENRY
          Where's your hat!

                    NANCY
          Nella said it embarrassed her. My
          earrings are freezing my ears! I've got
          to go! I can't stand it!

Nancy vanishes into the white out.

                    HENRY
          Wait! Shit!

Henry inches slowly to the edge of the narrow ridge and peers
over to find terrified and crying Stephanie peering upward
trying unsuccessfully to climb the ice wall.

                    HENRY (CONT'D)
          You gotta move back!

Henry slowly descends the ice wall with her skis, forcefully
ramming his ski boots into the wall with all his might.

One ski pole falls from the bundle and is quickly swept by
the wind, vanishing down a centuries old glacier crevice.
Both try not to look but Stephanie is panic stricken.

Henry throws the pole's mate off into the wind. It
accelerates away. Henry finally reaches Stephanie and assists
her with her skis.

EXT. MOUNTAIN TRAIL CERVINIA

Nancy fights against the driving wind and snow. She stops
and removes her diamond EARRINGS and throws them into the
wind, covering her painful ears for a moment. She removes
her skis and bravely continues trudging along in the waist
deep snow for her life.

EXT. TOP OF MOUNTAIN CREVASSE

                    HENRY
               (yelling)
          Stay on this path, I'll be right behind
          you.

                    STEPHANIE
          What if we fall?

                    HENRY
          We won't!

Henry is behind Stephanie waiting for her to go.

                    STEPHANIE
          I can't!

Henry spreads his legs slightly and skis directly behind
Stephanie, touching his pelvis to her butt as he puts his
arms around her body.

                    HENRY
          Now you can.

They ski carefully down the narrow path as one. Stephanie
looks fearfully to the right down a narrow crevasse. The
wind threatens them down the cliff.

                    HENRY (CONT'D)
          Just look straight ahead.

They slowly ski forward as a strong GUST battles to blow them
down the crevasse.

The warming hut is finally in sight. They quickly take their
skis off and run back up to the main trail and head into the
warmth.

INT. PEAK WARMING HUT - CERVINIA - LATE AFTERNOON

Students sit around with scared faces, no one is laughing or
drinking beer in the nearly deserted hut. Tom jumps up and
helps them in.

                    TOM
          Hey dude, sorry man, that was uncool
          leaving you.

                    HENRY
          Yeah...we just took a little detour.

Henry smiles at Stephanie. She appreciates his non
deprecation and is enamored with her new found hero.

                    NELLA
          Where's Nancy, isn't she with you!

                    HENRY
          No, fuck?! She said she couldn't wait.
          She didn't even have a hat.

Henry looks at Nella. Nella is nervous.

                    NELLA
          I bet she's down waiting for us.

INT. RED DRAGON LODGE-EVENING

Both groups are finally mingling. Stephanie sits extra close
to Henry as they joke about their close call. Nella comes in
concerned.

                    HENRY
          Any word?

                    NELLA
          I'll go check across the street.

Nella exits.

                    STEPHANIE
          I hope she's all right.

                    PATRICK
          We should have stayed together.

Nella enters the bar in more of a panic.

                    NELLA
          She's no where. We've got to tell the
          mountain.

Henry gets up and approaches the bar with Nella. The
bartender dials the phone, speaks and shakes his head toward
the group.

                    NELLA
          How much for a search party.

Nella gets out her CHECKBOOK and starts writing. The
bartender puts his hand over her checkbook.

                    BARTENDER
               (heavy accent)
          The storm is still very heavy. They can
          do nothing until morning.

Henry and Nella sit down with the group in despair.

                    NELLA
          This is all my fault. If I hadnt' been--

                    HENRY
          It's all our faults.

Henry touches Nella's shoulder.

                    PATRICK
          Let's go back to the Hotel and wait for
          her.

The group readies to leave.

INT. RED DRAGON LODGE ROOM - EARLY MORNING

The blinding sun wakes everyone who has spent the night in
the same room. Nella is asleep with the phone on her chest.
The group hurries to get dressed.

INT. GONDOLA PEAK HUT - MORNING

Nella, Henry, Patrick and Stephanie anxiously exit the
gondola and head outside into the blinding sun. They
approach a forlorn Italian Ski PATROL.

                    NELLA
          Have you seen our friend?

                    PATROL
               (heavy accent)
          We find her.

Nella beams.

                    NELLA
          I knew it!

A covered sled stretcher slides by the group. The patrolman
nods behind the sled. Nella's expression turns to horror.

                    NELLA
               (sobbing)
          Oh my God Nancy!

Nella runs to the stretcher and drops to her knees in agony.

> NELLA
> It's all my fault. Nancy!

A worker purposely drops a huge heavy box on top of the stretcher. Nella is horrified.

> PATROL
> (chuckling)
> No, she is over here.

The patrolman points up to a CHAIR LIFT HUT beyond the stretcher. Nancy pokes her matted bed hair head and bare shoulder out of the window.

> NANCY
> Hey you guys! Up here!

A smiling Italian stud sticks his head out and pulls her back inside. Nancy waves. The group smirks and is greatly relieved. Stephanie hugs and kisses Henry.

INT. ART BAR -FLORENCE - EVENING

Stephanie, Nella, Nancy and others quaff their Long Island Iced Teas in the old style bar that shows soundless 50's American cartoons on the wall.

> STEPHANIE
> Thank God for Henry.

> NANCY
> Nella, you need to give him another
> chance.

> NELLA
> So, OK, Mr. Hero was really cool and all
> to save you, maybe even to secretly have
> sex with, but he is still NOT dating
> material.

Nella examines her wedding ring finger.

> NELLA
> I mean, ewww! I'm so sure. The chance of
> a guy like that making enough money to
> support me are..sa-lih-him.

> STEPHANIE
> Mr. Hero? You know Nella, seems to me
> you haven't had much luck following your
> plan.
> (MORE)

                    STEPHANIE (cont'd)
          I mean, Stuart Stephenson, great, his
          parents own every shipyard in Seattle,
          but you said he used to hump your leg
          like a dog and come in five seconds.
          What is THAT?

                    NELLA
          Well, he was good to be seen with.

                    STEPHANIE
          But can you imagine if you married him?
          You'd have to scoop his goo off your leg
          with a turkey baster to get pregnant and
          buy a "Big John" dildo just to get off.

Stephanie makes a big "O" with her fist.

The other girls ROAR with laughter. Nella attempts to
instill her control for silence.

                    NELLA
          My, my, my. You're even starting to talk
          like them. Just don't come crying to me
          when you're living in that trailer in
          Walla Walla.

                    STEPHANIE
          At least we'll be in love. I think
          you're kind of jealous.

Stephanie is now the alpha female. Nella looks at the table,
busted.

                    NELLA
          Of what?

Henry walks up behind Stephanie and surprises her with a
kiss.

                    STEPHANIE
               (to Nella)
          That.

                    HENRY
          Hey sweetie, just wanted to see if you
          wanted to get some dinner with Tom and
          Kate.

                    STEPHANIE
          Sure.

Stephanie gets up and waves goodbye to the girls.

INT. TOM'S ROOM

Kate fiddles in the bathroom while Tom lays on the bed. She
pokes her head out holding a box of TAMPONS staring at Tom.
Tom nods at the tampons quizzically.

> TOM
> I'm pretty cool about a lot of things,
> but this boyfriend doesn't buy plugs at
> La Farmacia--

Kate hurls the box at Tom's head. He catches it.

> TOM
> Whoa! relax, Vowl-yo com-prar-ay un
> cartoline di plug--

> KATE
> --no dick. I haven't used them in two
> months.

> TOM
> So that's good right? No fuss or muss,
> save a little cash--

> KATE
> Last time this happened, I was pregnant.

> TOM
> Is that how it works?

Kate looks dejected at the bed.

> TOM
> So that means.

> KATE
> Yup.

> TOM
> Right on! You're the first one I've ever
> knocked up that I've loved.

Tom hops over to Kate and gets on one knee.

> TOM
> You're my number one babe ever Kate.
> Would you marry me?

> KATE
> Wouldn't it be easier to just hyper-space
> it and still hang out?

                    TOM
        But baby, I really love you. I don't
        want to zap our first born out of the
        galaxy.

                    KATE
        Guess I love you too.

They passionately kiss.

A KNOCK on the door.

Tom opens the door to SOAKING WET Henry and Stephanie.

                    TOM
        On ray! Dude! Guess what!?

Tom stands up and makes a curve over his belly.

                    HENRY
        Serious?

                    TOM
        As a heart attack. And I'm not going to
        throw her down the stairs or give her a
        hanger. We're getting married.

                    STEPHANIE
        Kate! That's wonderful.

                    HENRY
        Can I buy your baby a drink?

Henry grabs a towel off the bed and dries his hair quickly.
He puts the towel over Stephanie's hair like a nun's habit
and plants a kiss on her.

                    KATE
        Sure.

                    HENRY
        Better yet, I'll go get some vino and
        some mineral water for you.

Henry touches Kate's stomach. Henry puts on a trench coat,
and grabs an INSPECTOR CLOUSSEAU HAT and exits.

                    HENRY (CONT'D)
        Rad hat dude.

Tom nods.

                    TOM
        Got it at Cascini.

EXT. PENSIONE BELLETINI-FLORENCE

Henry bounces out of the high arched door into the POURING
RAIN. Bruised and beaten Al-Banri waits in the cafe just
across from the pensione. He grabs his backpack and follows
Henry.

Henry jukes left down a dark street. (suggest "Theme from
Pink Panther) Al-Banri stalks 30 feet behind. This is
finally his chance. He removes the SILENCER from his
backpack and steps to the other side of the street to
increase his angle. Henry's head appears in the SCOPE.

Henry spies a shiny gold COIN on the wet sidewalk.

                    HENRY
                (bad French accent)
        Inspector Clousseau, vat do we have here?

Henry leans over to pick up the coin as Al-Banri FIRES THE
GUN. The bullet embeds itself in a four foot thick stone
wall just above Henry's head with a PING.

Henry stands upright and merrily trots along. A group of
loud talking Italians approach Al-Banri from behind. He is
exasperated and furious. He darts away

Henry turns on yet another street. He spies a young man in
the doorway with his back turned, obviously making out with
someone. As Henry gets closer, he notices Patrick's A's hat
with the bill turned around.

                    HENRY   (CONT'D)
                (to himself)
            That dog.

Henry sneaks up behind him and tickles him vigorously under
his arms. Patrick swings around in terror. Henry notices he
has been kissing a handsome twenty something Italian MAN!

                    HENRY
            Uh, hey Patrick.

                    PATRICK
            What are you doing here?!

                    HENRY
            Taking a short cut. Ya gonna introduce
            me?

                    PATRICK
                (agitated)
            Henry...Marco... Marco...Henry. Ya seen
            enough?

> HENRY
> Hold up dude. I'm your bro. You think
> this is going to change anything?

Patrick is exasperated, rubbing his face and pulling at his
hair.

> PATRICK
> I was gonna tell you dude. I just
> couldn't.

> HENRY
> You're right. This is big.

> PATRICK
> I figured if my idol was proudly banging
> fat girls, the sky was the limit.

Henry hugs Patrick.

> HENRY
> So Marko, you speeka the English?

> MARCO
> Yes, little bit.

> HENRY
> Cool, vieni al' incontrare i miei amici.

Henry beckons to Marco. The three walk back with Marco in
the middle, smiling and eager to make friends.

EXT. PENSIONE BELLETINI-FLORENCE

Al-Banri lurks in the shadows waiting for Henry. Henry,
Marco and Patrick joke and laugh, bounding up the stairs of
the pensione.

> AL-BANRI
> (muttering)
> Ha ha. Laugh laugh. Everything always
> so funny. I show you funny.

Al-Banri reaches in his bag and puts on a billed hat. He
takes out several small wired items and a miniature
MICROPHONE.

INT. PENSION BELLETINI LOBBY - EVENING

Tom, Kate and Stephanie wait on the plush leather couches for
Henry's return. Henry and company enter the lobby.

                    STEPHANIE
          Patrizio. How you been? Where's the
          vino?

                    HENRY
          I've got a better idea. Let's go to Bocca
          Lupo. We've got alot to celebrate.

                    STEPHANIE
          And I have daddy's gold card for just
          such an emergency.

Stephanie pulls it out of her tight jeans and holds it like a
TV commercial.

                    TOM
          God I love hanging out with you Steff.

Tom gives her a hug and they exit.

EXT. PENSIONE BELLETINI

Al-Banri watches the group exit and sees his opportunity to
infiltrate the pensione.

INT. PENSIONE BELLETINI LOBBY

Al-Banri, dressed as a phone repairman, confidently enters
the lobby and looks for their phone. He walks to the phone;
puts down his backpack; unscrews the mouthpiece and begins to
implant a BUGGING DEVICE. Nella grumbles to the phone
holding a letter.

                    NELLA
          Um, excuse me! You going to be long?

Al-Banri is startled and agitated and drops a key piece of
equipment.

                    AL-BANRI
                (in Arabic)
          Listen you bitch! I should kill you
          right now.

                    NELLA
          Don't I know you?

Al-Banri realizes he must keep his cool and strains a quick
smile before quickly turning his face.

                    AL-BANRI
                (in English)
          Just a few more minutes my fine lady.

Nella turns around confused. Al-Banri finishes up. Nella grabs the phone. Al-Banri has his head pointed down.

                    AL-BANRI
          Here you are.

Nella dials the phone. Al-Banri looks back and then runs out of the pensione.

                    NELLA
          Hi it's me.

Nella makes a face. YELLING ensues from the other line. She holds it away from her ear.

                    NELLA
          Oh my God! Would you calm down. Maybe
          you can make a donation or something.

Nella holds the phone out from the YELLING.

INT. HOTEL ROOM - FLORENCE

Al-Banri still huffing from his run, jerks the headphones away from his head to avoid Nella's fathers yelling. The phone HANGS UP in his ear.

Al-Banri hears a new VOICE talking. He listens with interest.

INT. PENSIONE BELLETINI LOBBY

Adriane casually speaks on the phone.

                    ADRIANE
          ....yes Mom. Non stop from London,
          flight 181, and Henry too. Trust me mom,
          he doing great. God Mom, yes, I'm still
          a virgin. What a question.

Adriane rolls her eyes.

INT. HOTEL ROOM - FLORENCE

Al-Banri does his version of the witch's brew DANCE.

                    AL-BANRI
          Woo-Hoo! I finally got him.

INT. BOCCA LUPO RESTAURANT

Tom, Kate, Stephanie, Henry, Patrick and Marco sit in a window seat in the upscale trattoria.

                         TOM
          Dude, one time I went over this HUGE jump
          on my BMX and landed and the seat fell
          off, and I didn't know it, and WHAM! I
          don't see how you guys do it--

Kate shakes her head at her fiance.

                         PATRICK
          But were you in love with your BMX bike?

                         TOM
          Totally.

Nella lumbers by the window in tears. Stephanie catches her
eye and motions her in. Nella enters.

                         STEPHANIE
          Sweetie, what's the matter?

Stephanie hugs Nella.

                         NELLA
          Dad found out I'm flunking Italian. He
          said if I don't pass I have to finish up
          school in Slow-Can. That awful place
          you're from.

                         HENRY
          It'll be good for you.

                         NELLA
          You don't understand. A girl like me
          would die up there.

                         HENRY
          Me getting you busted didn't help. I
          could teach you a few tricks--

                         NELLA
          Would you?!

                         MARCO
          I can help too.

Nella looks at Marco hornily. Patrick shocks her by kissing
Marco. Nella starts to interject.

                         HENRY
          Now concentrate.

TIME PASSES

Empty plates and carafes litter the table. Nella points to
herself.

                    NELLA
          Ho.

Nella assures Henry.

                    NELLA
          Even though I'm not really one.

Nella waves.

                    NELLA
          Hai.

Nella holds her stomach in a fake laugh.

                    NELLA
          Ha. I have, you have, and the important
          person has...I get it!

                    HENRY
          And you can sit next to me tomorrow.
          We'll get it done.

                    NELLA
          Oh Henry.

Nella smacks a wet one on Henry. Henry wipes it off.

                    NELLA
          I had you all wrong.

INT. PHONE BOOTH - SPOKANE - MORNING

Tabitha open mouth kisses the glass of the phone booth while
Needa tries to pay attention on the phone. Riva is smashed
to one side bemused by Tabitha.

                    RIVA
          She has very big mouth.

                    NEEDA
          How can you let Al-Banri do this. It is
          our mission now.

INT. ABU'S OFFICE - EVENING

                    ABU
          He is already in London building the
          portable stereo bomb for his flight.

INTERCUT AS NEEDED

                    NEEDA
               (in Arabic)
          I must put bomb on plane!

Riva can't believe his ears.

                    ABU
          OK...OK. But no fancy hotels and excuses
          as Al-Banri has done.

Riva looks at Needa perplexed and worried.

INT. CLASSROOM - DAY

Henry sits near Nella amid students completing their tests.
Henry looks on her paper while Mrs. Baldini paces the other
direction and quickly jots down a few answers. He gives
Nella the "ok" sign to the rest of her answers. Nella beams
as she quickly erases his answers and replaces them in her
handwriting.

INT. HALLWAY

Nella hugs Henry tightly and SQUEALS.

                    NELLA
          We did it!

                    HENRY
          You did it, kinda.

Bruno waddles up holding the completed impressive BUST of
Henry.

                    BRUNO
          You got your "A", aren't you going to
          take this home?

                    HENRY
          You keep it. I want you to remember me.

                    BRUNO
          I couldn't forget you even if I wanted
          to. "Mary with a cherry".

Henry and Bruno emotionally hug with Henry's BUST in the way.

                    HENRY
          Can I buy you a shot tonight?

                    BRUNO
          Seeing as they are all free.

Stephanie walks out with her beautifully finished and
repaired EAGLE and hands it to Bruno who struggles to hold
both pieces of art.

>   STEPHANIE
>   Save mine till we come back on our
>   honeymoon.

>   BRUNO
>   You got it.

Henry and Stephanie walk out arm in arm.

INT. HENRY'S ROOM

Stephanie lays on top of Henry passionately kissing him.

>   HENRY
>   You're kidding me. So I was just a "bet"
>   for Melody.

>   STEPHANIE
>   I lost $20.

Henry shakes his head and smiles.

>   STEPHANIE
>   My family is going to love you. So just
>   a couple more things.

Henry looks at the ceiling.

>   STEPHANIE (cont'd)
>   No more dick jokes, the fart jokes are
>   only funny sometimes, and never, ever say
>   the "c" word--

>   HENRY
>   Caro mia?

>   STEPHANIE
>   That one's OK. And shave this better.

Stephanie rubs his chin. Henry rolls Stephanie over.

>   HENRY
>   I thought you liked it?

Henry shakes his head left to right and GROWLS.

>   STEPHANIE
>   I like that part, but I swear you're
>   gonna give me a rash.

> HENRY
> (singing a la Partridge
> Family)
> Ba-ba-ba-ba-ba-ba-ba-ba-ba-bah-buh-ba-ba-
> baaah..

Stephanie looks at him curiously. Henry begins to playfully
tear off his clothes, and then hers.

> HENRY
> (still singing)
> I'm sleeping, and right in the middle of
> a good dream, when all at once I wake up,
> from something that keeps knocking at my
> brain...before I go insane, I hold my
> pillow to my head.

Henry pulls off his last stitch of clothing. He kneels back
naked over his prize, his butt in full view.

> HENRY
> ...and spring up in my bed, screaming out
> the words I dread. I THINK I LOVE YOU!

> STEPHANIE
> (returning song)
> I know I love you.

They get down to business.

INT. BOCCA LUPO RESTAURANT - EVENING

A BANNER reads: FAREWELL GONZAGINIS

As in the opening scenes, the Gonzaginis, party like rock
stars at their farewell dinner. Henry admires his ugly
American award STEIN with Stephanie by his side.

Melody walks up and stuffs a wad of bills in Henry's shirt
pocket and pats it.

> MELODY
> I thought half was only fair.

Melody winks and grabs her Italian man by the hand and slinks
back in the crowd. Henry smiles and shakes his head, happy
to have the cash.

                                        CUT TO:

INT. LONDON AIRPORT - DAY

As in the opening scene, 25 feet away, Riva and Needa
intently observe Henry walking to an insurance kiosk.

Henry deposits the money in an envelope and trots back to
Stephanie.

                    STEPHANIE
          I'm sure the insurance company will thank
          you.

Henry lies down, and puts his head in Stephanie's lap, as in
the opening scenes. He closes his eyes. Stephanie closes
hers too.

TIME PASSES

Out the terminal window, a CLOSE UP of a TOSHIBA BOOM BOX
with AIR MALTA tags rides a black conveyor belt.

                    ANNOUNCER (O.S.)
          Flight 181 non stop service to Seattle is
          now ready for pre boarding, please--

We notice Needa holding a BLACK BOOM BOX.

                    RIVA
          Let us go now to tell him he is safe.

                    NEEDA
          He will think we are crazy person! You
          know we are more than dead if Abu finds
          out we do this.

Needa realizes what's he's holding.

                    NEEDA
          Let's get rid of this now.

                    ANNOUNCER (O.S.)
          Flight 181 non stop service to Seattle
          will be delayed on hour.---

Riva and Needa walk right past Adriane in the DUTY FREE SHOP.

INT. AIRPORT TERMINAL - BACK ROOM

Riva and Needa carefully dismantle the explosives.

                    NEEDA
          Careful, this is not play dough.

Riva throws away half the stereo in one bin, half in the
adjacent bin, covering them both with boxes and papers. They
quickly exit, and re-enter the terminal near the DUTY FREE
SHOP.

INT. DUTY FREE SHOP

Adriane carefreely drops items in to her overloaded basket.
She approaches the clerk.

                    ADRIANE
          What a great name for a store, because it
          is *such* not a "duty" to shop here.

Adriane admires her mounds of goods being rung up by the
clerk who ignores her. She looks at her watch.

                    ADRIANE
          Oh my God!

Adriane runs out of the store leaving her merchandise on the
counter. She watches her plane pull away. On the benches,
she notices Henry and Stephanie fast asleep. They have all
missed their flight.

Henry is restlessly saying, "I love you", in his sleep.

Adriane approaches them. Henry wakes up in a panic and looks
around. He sees Stephanie and hugs her.

                    HENRY
          I just had the scariest fucking dream.

                    ADRIANE
          We missed our flight.

                    HENRY
          I don't care. Whoa.

INT. LIVING ROOM - SPOKANE - MORNING

Alice fluffs the pillows of her couch. A DING sounds from
the kitchen.

INT. KITCHEN

Alice scurries to remove Henry's favorite cookies from the
oven. In the background, her small TV plays the newsbreak.

                    NEWSMAN (ON TV)
          It has been confirmed that a jumbo-jet
          headed for Seattle exploded over Scotland-
          -

The TV shows the wreckage site. Alice is in shock. The
phone rings. Alice is in a shock. Alice picks up the phone,
and says nothing.

> HENRY
> (on telephone)

Mom!

Alice sinks to the ground and cries tears of relief.

INT. ABU'S OFFICE

Abu holds Al-Banri in front of him. The HERALD lies on the desk, it reads: 747 JUMBO EXPLODES IN SKY.

> ABU
> We are lucky to have you. Allah will
> deal with Riva and Needa for their
> desertion.

> AL-BANRI
> I never trusted them sir. You can trust--

Another recruit runs in holding a radio.

> RADIO
> "The same organization responsible for
> the Rome and Vienna attacks has claimed
> responsibility for this heinous assault"

Abu looks at Al-Banri, realizing Abu lied to him and smacks him hard repeatedly with his paper.

SUPER: ONE YEAR LATER

INT. BEDROOM - SPOKANE

A black male hand puts a Coke can on a night stand. A light blue mechanic's shirt hangs on a bedpost with a red and white patch that reads, "BIG JOHN". The bed rocks and SQUEAKS.

> NELLA (O.S.)
> Oh Yeah! I'm never going back.

The bed continues to BANG and SQUEAK.

> NELLA (O.S.) (CONT'D)
> So...(panting)you used to be an actor?
> What kind of movies?

> BIG JOHN
> (gruff deep black voice)
> I don't think you'd of seen any of these.
> They got into merchandising me towards
> the end. GRUNT

                    NELLA
          That's great. So they made actions
          figures out of you? PANT

                    BIG JOHN
          Uh, well...of part of me.

INT. SPAGHETTI WESTERN RESTAURANT - FLORENCE - EVENING

Patrick pours a beer behind a bar as Marco seats people.
Marco looks over and blows Patrick a macho kiss as Patrick
winks back.

                    HENRY (O.S.)
          Patrick decided to stay back and
          capitalize on the tourists.

A young western patron walks up to the bar and speaks to
Patrick.

                    PATRICK
          Two Heinekens and two burgers coming
          right up. Would you like to Grande size
          those for 2000 lire more?

The patron turns his hand up in approval to Patrick.

MATCH CUT: UPTURNING HAND

INT. CHURCH - SPOKANE - AFTERNOON

A priest UPTURNS his HAND to the church. The entire gang,
including Tom, Kate and Bart, stand in church pews looking
ahead. On the altar, Needa and Tabitha face the crowd with
Riva and Adriane by their sides. Henry and Samantha deal
with their SCREAMING new baby in the front pew.

                    PRIEST
          I present to you, Mr. and Mrs. Sabri.

Needa and Tabitha kiss. The church erupts in APPLAUSE. Riva
kisses both cheeks of Needa in embrace.

                    RIVA
          My girl is virgin.

Riva winks at Adriane embracing Tabitha. Adriane twinkles
her fingers at Riva.

                    HENRY (O.S.)
          Now he's officially an American. See,
          we're not so bad, if you just give us a
          chance.

INT. L'ANGELO AZZURO BAR - FLORENCE - EVENING

Bruno stands with a stopwatch in front of 80 new super drunk laughing students.

                    BRUNO
         OK...number 72! Shoot 'em!

Bruno laughs and shakes his head. He winks at a smiling coed.

EXT. L'ANGELO AZZURO BAR

Padre Via stands, hands in pockets, looking in the window at the mayhem. He pulls his hands out, stretches them to the heavens, shakes his head walks away.

SUPER:

ON DECEMBER 21, 1988, PAN AM FLIGHT 103 EXPLODED OVER LOCKERBIE, SCOTLAND KILLING ALL 259 PEOPLE ON BOARD. MORE THAN HALF OF THEM WERE AMERICAN COLLEGE STUDENTS STUDYING ABROAD RETURNING HOME.

WHILE THE BLAME WAS PLACED SQUARELY ON THE LIBYAN GOVERNMENT, THE REAL PERPETRATOR WAS MOST LIKELY ABU-NIDAL, A DISPLACED PALESTINIAN LIVING IN LIBYA IN 1987, WHOSE MONEYED PARENTS WERE KILLED IN A JEWISH UPRISING DURING THE BRITISH OCCUPATION IN THE 40'S. IN 2002 HE WAS FOUND DEAD IN IRAQ FROM AN APPARENT SUICIDE, WITH FOUR BULLET WOUNDS TO HIS HEAD.

TWO SUSPECTED LIBYANS WERE TRIED. ONLY ONE WAS CONVICTED AND SENTENCED TO TWENTY YEARS. MANY BELIEVE HE HAD NOTHING TO DO WITH IT.

THE LIBYAN GOVERNMENT RECENTLY PURCHASED A $500,000 HOME IN THE UPMARKET SUBURB OF GLASGOW, ENGLAND TO ALLOW THE PRISONER'S FAMILY TO VISIT THEIR COUNTRY'S SACRIFICIAL LAMB.

                              FADE OUT:

ROLL CREDITS: SUGGEST "WALKING ON THE SPOT" CROWDED HOUSE

www.ingramcontent.com/pod-product-compliance
Lightning Source LLC
Chambersburg PA
CBHW080837250626
47160CB00009B/2971